THE HOUSEGUEST

Hope you enjoy the book.

Best wishes

Eve Graham

BY
E M GRAHAM

Grosvenor House
Publishing Limited

The right of E M Graham to be identified as the author of this
work has been asserted by her in accordance with Section 78
of the Copyright, Designs and Patents Act 1988

The book cover picture is copyright to Inmagine Corp LLC

This book is published by
Grosvenor House Publishing Ltd
28-30 High Street, Guildford, Surrey, GU1 3EL.
www.grosvenorhousepublishing.co.uk

A CIP record for this book
is available from the British Library

ISBN 978-1-78148-902-4

CHAPTER 1

BLUEBELL COTTAGE

Friday afternoon, Kim was cleaning out the post- op kennels. She had worked at the vets for four years now. When she started it was part time, ten hours a week, but two months ago, not really through choice, it became a full time position. When she had finished and everything had been disinfected, she placed clean blankets in the kennels ready for the next patients. She looked out of the window. It was a complete 'white out' and the snow had been falling steadily all day. "A typical Highland February", she thought.

Just then Stan, the ageing vet came in to the room saying, "I think you'd better head for home Kim, we don't want you getting stuck in a snowdrift". He explained that he had been listening to the radio and some minor roads had already been closed due to drifting snow. Kim normally worked until four thirty answering the phone etc. Stan said he would hold the fort and also get some paper work done at the same time. Kim liked Stan; he was her favourite out of the three vets who worked at the practice. He was an old fashioned sort of vet who should have retired by now but loved his work too much to give it up.

His son Steven was also in the practice but Steven's god was money. Kim could remember the time when a young woman came in carrying a cat. The cat was in a dreadful state. She explained that she had hit the cat with her car. All Steven seemed to be interested in was who would pay for its treatment. There followed a somewhat heated argument during which the woman threatened to contact the local newspapers exposing Stevens lack of compassion. Not wanting any bad publicity he took the cat from her. As it turned out the cat's injuries were so bad that the poor creature had to be put to sleep.

Kim thanked Stan and saying goodbye, set off for home. As she got into her car she was glad it had four wheel drive, she would certainly be using it today. Her home was out in the country, fifteen miles from the town. The main road was not too bad but when she turned off onto the minor road she found herself having to go at a snails pace. In some parts if it had not been for the fence on either side, she would not have been able to tell what was road and what was fields. Still, she loved living in this part of Scotland. In the summer it was a beautiful drive home.

Her husband Tom had carved out a successful career buying and selling property. You needed to be competitive and Tom drove a hard bargain and could be quite ruthless when he wanted something. This was how they had managed to get Bluebell Cottage. When it had came on the market Tom, Kim and baby Nicola were living in a large house in town. Little Adam had not came along at this point.

When she and Tom first saw the property, they were told an old lady had lived in the house for the last forty years and the building was in need of lots of TLC. When she died the house came on to the market and her only surviving relative was a niece who lived in America. Tom offered the woman a fixed price, considerably below what the cottage would have fetched on the open market. She accepted and as they say, the rest is history. That was twenty years ago.

She would never forget that spring afternoon, when they had come to view the property. Turning up the long drive, it was apparent how the cottage had got its name. A two-acre plot of mixed woodland surrounded the house. The floor was carpeted with vivid blue wild hyacinth. Kim had fallen in love with location immediately. There was a large gravel parking area, in front of the two-storey building. Above the doorway, the date 1897 was carved into the lintel. Adjacent to the house were two stone-built, single storey outbuildings each of which had a corrugated iron roof. One was large enough to be used for a garage: the other was currently being used as a woodshed. Before going inside, they checked the rear of the property.

An ancient privet hedge surrounded the extensive garden. There were numerous shrubs and flowers, resulting in a blaze of colour and a heavenly mixture of scents. Beside the large lawn was an even larger vegetable plot, long since over grown. Weeds towered where once vegetables had been grown. Nettles, brambles, docks and wild roses covered the ground. If they decided to buy the property, they would have their work cut out reclaiming the garden from nature. Just beyond the privet hedge, there were numerous fruit trees. At a glance Kim could see apple, plum, cherry and pear trees. On closer inspection she was delighted to see blackcurrant, redcurrant, gooseberry bushes as well as raspberries. She immediately thought of home-made jams and chutneys. The old lady had obviously been a bird lover, as empty bird feeders hung throughout the garden.

On entering the hallway, Kim could not resist opening the door and peeping in to the rather dark cupboard beneath the staircase. Turning left, they entered the sitting room. The first thing that caught Kim's eye was a beautiful old cast-iron fireplace, surrounded by ornate tiles in a beautiful floral pattern. The high mantelpiece was made of solid oak. The hearth was a large slab of grey Caithness slate. Next the couple went into the kitchen. Apart from a double Belfast sink, the only other fixtures were a few shelves on the walls. This room, like most farmhouse kitchens was large, with plenty of space for a dining area. The view from the window overlooked the vast rear garden. The last room downstairs was a small room at the front of the property, possibly used at one time as a spare bedroom. Tom thought it would make an ideal study. Finally they checked out the upstairs of the house. This consisted of three quaint bedrooms with coombed ceilings and a small bathroom. Out of all the rooms, the bathroom required the most attention. The old bath was badly chipped and the hand basin was cracked, but they knew the house was for them.

As she drove on she thought how nice it would be if Tom were at home to welcome her. 'Stop it' she told herself. He had been gone for three months now and he wasn't coming back. He was finding himself with a tribe of bloody hippies in their weird commune. What had gone wrong? Twenty-six years of marriage, two children and now nothing.

Her eldest, a daughter Nicola, was in New Zealand and had no intentions of coming home. She had met her New Zealander here and then went over there for a holiday and never came back again. That was over a year ago. Yes, she kept in touch with a phone call every fortnight and sometimes a letter in between. In fact her daughter kept in touch more from the other side of the world than her son Adam, who was only forty miles away. Adam was at university, enjoying a carefree bachelor life. How she missed them all.

Deep in thought she crawled along the treacherous little road. She had been on autopilot and didn't really remember the last five or six miles. Isn't it funny how you can drive for miles without being aware of driving and it is only when something catches your attention that you come back to the controls. It could be a rabbit or another car. In Kim's case it was a solitary figure that appeared through the blizzard.

Tom and Kim had shared everything together. They had been a close-knit family. The children, perhaps because they were slightly isolated, spent a lot of time with their parents and shared their love for the country. Camping, walking and lots of picnics at local beauty spots: but not the popular well-known ones where everyone went: special places known only to them. They had two dogs, both rescued from the local dog home. One was a collie cross and the other was a spaniel. The dogs were inseparable and, of course, went everywhere with the family.

Tom had his own business as an estate agent and financial advisor. Kim had stayed at home to look after the family and maintain their extensive garden. When the children left home to go their separate ways, Kim decided to take a part time job. She loved animals so becoming a veterinary nurse seemed like the natural choice. Although sometimes upsetting, for the most part it was a fulfilling and rewarding job. It was through working there that her last dog had come into her life. Pepsi was an old collie whose owner had died and the dog was not wanted by any the remaining relatives.

Kim had been on duty the day he was brought into the surgery to be put down. The old man's son handed the dog over to Kim. As she led him through to the consulting room she was touched at how trusting and gentle the old dog was as he padded along beside her. Once inside the room Kim bent down and looked into Pepsis eyes, her heart melted. She had taken many dogs to meet their fate but usually there was a good reason, ill health or aggression. These she could accept, but old

Pepsi's only crime was that, he had no one to look after him in his twilight years. Kim turned to Stan, who was preparing the injection. "I'll take him home, he doesn't look as if he'll be any trouble" she said. And so Pepsi went home with Kim that day which was three years ago. Stan reckoned Pepsi was about 11 when Kim saved his life. For the next three years Pepsi never put a paw wrong. It was as if he spent the next three years thanking Kim for what she'd done. He never left her side and was completely devoted to her. Two months after Tom walked out of her life, Pepsi left too. She woke up one morning to find he had passed away in the night. Kim felt that everything she loved was being taken away from her. At the time she felt that Pepsi's death was the last straw. But life goes on and so had Kim, though at times in an automatic daze.

Kim, on seeing the figure in the snow, was brought abruptly back to the present. "My God" she thought, "poor soul out in this weather". As she pulled up, the figure turned around. It was a tall, slim woman carrying a baby, wrapped in blankets. Immediately Kim leaned across and opened the passenger door. "Can I give you lift?" she enquired. Without hesitation the woman climbed into the jeep. She was completely soaked and covered with snow. As she opened the blanket, to Kim's amazement, it wasn't a baby but a little white dog. The woman introduced herself as Janu and had an unusual accent. She told Kim she had been on her way to visit her boyfriend, when her car had become stuck in the snow. So she had decided to walk to try to find a phone. At the time, Kim found nothing strange in her explanation. She asked Janu what her dog was called. "Gemini" she replied. "Unusual name", she thought and there was something else unusual about Gemini, he had the most piercing pale blue eyes she had ever seen: his owner had the same piercing eyes. Janu was tall, blonde and beautiful. She was probably in her mid thirties and dressed in what Kim would describe as new age hippie clothes.

CHAPTER 2

ELYSIUM

"What a joke", she thought, "here she was helping the enemy; the type of person who brain washed her Tom." Actually she should have seen it coming. She remembered how Tom decided on their silver wedding anniversary that he would take her away for a special weekend. Their anniversary was on the eighteenth of June, which that year, landed on a Wednesday. He told her he had booked them in from Friday the twentieth until Monday the twenty-third and that was all he would say about it, except that she would have a wonderful experience. "What about Pepsi?" she insisted, "Pepsi would be made welcome too" was Tom's reply. It may have been woman's intuition but Kim never felt good about the weekend. She just didn't want to go, although she could think of no good reason why.

On that sunny June morning, Tom, Kim and of course Pepsi, set off. Tom said it was a three-hour drive; they would stop en route for lunch and to give Pepsi a short walk. Around noon they came to a halt. They had been heading northwest and Tom had still not disclosed their final destination. After a pleasant bar lunch they set off again. An hour later they turned up a private drive. Kim saw a sign at the gateway with a single word 'ELYSIUM'. After a short distance the drive became little more than a dirt track that seemed to go on forever. Ancient pines and dense woodland lined the road that became narrower and rougher the further on they drove. Every type of tree Kim knew seemed to be on either side of the track, oak, beech, birch, ash, scots pine and chestnut. Finally they arrived outside what had once been a classy Victorian mansion, although years of neglect had taken its toll. The paint was peeling from the windows, some of the glass panels were cracked and others were missing altogether, with boards where they had been. The stonework was crumbling; in places grass and weeds were growing out of the guttering. Kim's heart sank "you must be joking" she said. Tom, looking rather peeved, told her to give it a chance, after all "looks are only skin deep" he said, which was one of Kim's favourite sayings. Tom's enthusiasm was apparent as he leapt from the car. Kim and Pepsi reluctantly followed, Pepsi seemed to sense Kim's mood, as he kept even closer than ever beside her. All around the house people were milling around, couples, groups and singles. It was their dress which caught Kim's eye; they all looked as though they had just stepped out of the sixties.

CHAPTER 3

THE FIRST NIGHT

Kim pulled up at the cottage. Thankfully she had set the heating on the timer and the house would be warm to come home to. Janu and Gemini followed her indoors. She suggested Janu have a hot shower to warm her up. She was sure she could find a pair of joggers and sweatshirt that she could borrow until they got her clothes dried out.

While Janu was in the shower Gemini sat immediately outside the bathroom door like a statue. Meanwhile Kim lit the log fire in the lounge. Once this was done she tapped on the bathroom door to say she would leave the clothes on the floor outside, but before she even touched the door, it opened, Janu stood there completely naked. Kim thrust the clothes towards her and turned away muttering she'd put the kettle on for a hot drink.

As she filled the kettle and got some mugs out of the cupboard, the picture of Janu standing naked flashed through her mind. She had the body of an athlete, she thought. Unlike herself, who after having turned forty seemed to struggle like most woman to keep in shape. There had been a time when she had been proud of her hourglass figure and had worn clothes to accentuate it. Now baggy sweatshirts were the order of the day. Since Toms departure she had began comfort eating as well as drinking a lot more. She found that a few glasses of wine in the evening helped her sleep better: at least that's what she told herself.

CHAPTER 4

GORDA AND SONNETTA

She wondered if Tom ever had a glass of wine at the commune or was it forbidden. There certainly had been none evident the weekend she'd been there. As a matter of fact, there hadn't been much of anything; sparse would have been an exaggeration in describing Elysium. As they approached the door, a couple appeared in the doorway. They were both dressed in green robes and around their necks hung pendants; Kim could make out that the spherical discs were little replicas of the planet earth. The man looked about fifty, he had long grey hair tied in a ponytail and the woman looked much older maybe in her seventies. She had the same long hair almost white which was in pigtails either side of her head. "Welcome Tom, so nice to see you again" said the man. Kim wondered where Tom had met this weirdo and why had he never mentioned it to her. He then turned to Kim, "Ah this must be your wonderful wife. My name is Gorda, and this is my soul mate Sonnetta". Gorda then embraced Kim and kissed her on the cheek. Kim could feel herself stiffen; she already felt uncomfortable and was not into this cuddling crap. Meanwhile Sonnetta was giving Tom the same welcome. Sonnetta then approached Kim who dodged sideways saying she must take Pepsi for a walk.

As she rounded the building she was amazed to see three full sized tepees. There were also numerous normal tents as well as a strange circular construction. She would later be told this was a yurt. She wandered around feeling very much like a tourist. She saw lots of little groups some singing and playing musical instruments. Perhaps the strangest sight was people who seemed to be hugging trees. That's it; I'm out of here, she thought, as she headed back to find Tom. She would tell Tom she wanted to go to the nearest B&B, or failing that, home.

CHAPTER 5

TEA FOR TWO

The click of the kettle brought her back to the present. At the same time she became acutely aware of a presence behind her. Turning quickly expecting to see Janu, she found Gemini sitting in the doorway watching her. The little dog made Kim feel uneasy which was surprising as she worked with dogs everyday. "I need a glass of wine," she said aloud, reaching into the fridge for a bottle. Janu spoke "Let me make you some herbal tea, you shouldn't pollute your body with all those chemicals". Janu then rummaged through her rucksack and produced a tin and began to make the tea. Kim stood watching her, feeling rather put out. She was asking herself, why she didn't just say, "No thank you I'd rather have wine".

As the tea was brewing Kim checked herself for over-reacting. Had she forgotten how to treat guests, after all she hadn't had much of a social life since Tom left. There were no dinners with friends no nights out at the local, no nothing in fact. The invitations stopped when she became a single woman. The married couples didn't like single women: the wives looked on them as competition and the husbands looked on them as prey.

To break the silence, Kim suggested Janu used the phone to contact her boyfriend, as he must be getting worried about her whereabouts, especially with the adverse weather conditions. Leading Janu into the sitting room, she pointed out the phone. Janu thanked her and began to dial. To give her some privacy she went into Tom's study. She could still make out the one-sided conversation and despite herself, listened intently. She heard her tell her boyfriend what had happened and that a kind passer by had taken her home to her house. There was a short silence, presumably as the boyfriend spoke. She heard her say goodbye and hang up. Kim went to the window to close the curtains, as it was now pitch black outside. The snow was falling even more heavily now and beginning to swirl, as the wind started to pick up. Again she had the strange feeling of being watched and sure enough when she turned around there was Gemini in the doorway. Kim decided to try to win the little dogs affection. "Come here Gemini! Come on pup!" she said. The dog ignored her and remained like a statue with his piercing blue eyes fixed upon her. Kim felt a shiver run down her spine. "I'm cracking up", she thought. Just then Janu called from the kitchen –"Tea's ready!". Gemini turned and trotted towards the sound. As Kim entered the kitchen a beautiful sweet scented aroma greeted her. Janu handed her a steaming mug of herbal tea. Both women then retired to sitting room. Janu sat down on the armchair beside the fire, Kim sat directly across from her on the sofa.

Kim asked her where her boyfriend lived and offered to give her a lift there in the morning, as due to the weather conditions, there would be no way of travelling there that night. Gemini meantime sat at Janu's feet staring straight ahead. Kim began to sip the tea. She had never really been one for herbal teas, which she found were normally over-priced and in her opinion, did no more good than Tetley tea bags. As she sipped the tea she was pleasantly surprised, it tasted sweet yet at the same time spicy. The more she drank, the more she relaxed. In fact, she couldn't remember when she last felt so relaxed. After all, the last year had been a drain. Her marriage had become more of a habit than anything else. Well, weren't most couples the same after more than quarter of a century? The weekend at Elysium had been the catalyst. It wasn't, that the hippies hadn't been friendly towards her: quite the reverse. They were sickly sweet.

CHAPTER 6

MISGIVINGS

The phone ringing broke her reverie. Kim tried to get up to answer the phone but was overcome by a wave of nausea. Janu jumped up and rushed to her side, "are you OK?" she asked. Meanwhile the answering machine clicked on. Kim explained she felt tired and also a bit queasy. "Put your feet up on the couch, I'll go and get you a glass of water", said Janu.

While Janu was in the kitchen, Kim glanced at the clock it was ten past six. The phone call had probably been Tina, one of the nurses from the practice. Tina was single, she was younger than Kim, probably in her late twenties, Kim reckoned. Earlier in the week they had agreed to meet for lunch on Saturday. Tina's lease was about to run out in the flat she was renting. She had been looking for new accommodation and Kim had suggested moving in with her for a trial period. Kim had considered this proposition very carefully before mentioning it to Tina. After all maybe some company was just what she needed. The fact they worked different shifts would mean they would both have their own space, and, the extra money would come in handy.

Kim opened her eyes: the room was empty except for Gemini. He was now sitting at the side of the settee staring at her. Kim's mouth felt uncomfortably dry, how long does it take to fill a glass of water, she thought impatiently. Glancing again at the clock, ten minutes had passed. "What had Janu done? Gone outside to collect snow and melt it?"

Still looking at the clock she began to realize the hands on the clock were the wrong way round, it didn't say ten past six it said half past two. "That can't be right!" she thought. "Eight and a half hours! Where had eight and a half hours gone?" She again began to rise. At this, Gemini leapt up onto the settee and began to bark. This little dog was beginning to piss her off, big time. She was trying to push him off when Janu appeared in the doorway. "How are you feeling, I was beginning to get worried about you", she said. "I feel like shit," croaked Kim. "Maybe coming down with a virus" replied Janu. At this she produced another mug of tea from the teapot sitting on the hearth. Kim sipped the hot sweet liquid, which soothed her dry throat. After another sip, Kim stretched over to put the mug on the coffee table beside the settee. She misjudged the distance and the mug tumbled to the floor. "Oh shit," exclaimed Kim getting up, thankfully not feeling any nausea, only a little dizzy. "Typical", she thought, "I just cleaned this carpet the other day". Janu looked somewhat annoyed. Then as quickly as the look of annoyance appeared, it was replaced with one of concern. "I'll get a cloth from the kitchen and clean up the mess. Then I will get you another mug of tea". "No thanks" said Kim "I'm going to get a glass of milk and I don't care what the time is I'm going to have a bath". Janu began to insist, but Kim refused to be told for the second time what to drink in her own house. In a change of strategy, Janu offered to run the bath.

Once in her warm bubble bath with the door locked, Kim began to relax. She began to ponder over the day's events. She was beginning to wish she had never picked up the woman and her dog. There was definitely something very strange about both of them. Lying back in her warm bath she began to think about the weekend again.

CHAPTER 7

THE INNER SANCTUM

Meeting Janu had brought back painful memories, like the huge argument she'd had with Tom. Sonnetta had intervened saying, "Come inside before you upset the balance" "What bloody balance" Kim had said. As far as she was concerned she was the only balanced person there. By this time a number of people had stopped what they were doing to watch the spectacle. Kim was furious. She was outnumbered and cornered, so reluctantly she went into the house. The inside of the property was in a dreadful state, paint peeling, damp patches on the walls and doors hanging off their hinges: all in all, a complete mess. The only pleasant thing was the smell of incense, which burned everywhere. This was presumably to disguise the smell of damp and decay.

Sonnetta led them upstairs to a large room. Inside Gorda sat cross-legged on the floor. Multi coloured candles surrounded him. Unlike the other rooms in the house, which had no floor covering, he sat on a luxurious carpet.

Other items of furniture, that were lacking everywhere else, were in no short supply here. He signalled for everyone to be seated on the floor in front of him. After what seemed like an eternity Gorda finally spoke.

He explained to Kim that Tom had been chosen because he was special, that they should give up their lives in the capitalist world, sell up their properties and invest their money in Elysium. They would then be part of the Fellowship and on the true path. Throughout this lecture, Kim kept glancing at Tom to see his reaction, but unlike Kim, he seemed totally fixated: almost hypnotised by Gorda. Kim had read about weird cults in America, but not here in Scotland. It was virtually unheard of. After about an hour the discussion ended, Gorda then dismissed them. Sonnetta showed them to their room and told them dinner would be at 7.30 p.m.

CHAPTER 8

STRANGE VOICES

Kim got out of the bath put on her robe then went downstairs. Janu and Gemini were sitting by the fire, Kim suddenly felt ravenous: she hadn't eaten since lunchtime. She asked Janu if she would like something to eat. She declined, saying she'd eaten some fruit while Kim slept. Kim went into the kitchen and looked in the fridge. She took out some cooked ham and made a sandwich. Feeling like something hot, she made a cup-a-soup. Looking out of the window, she noticed the snow had finally stopped. "Thank God!" she thought. "I'll get rid of them tomorrow". Janu came into the room and picked up the empty soup sachet. She began to read the ingredients all the while tutting and shaking her head. Kim decided to ignore her behaviour; after all, she wasn't the one drinking it. Kim went to the cupboard under the stairs to retrieve Pepsi's old bed. "You can use this for Gemini." she said, handing it to Janu, who took the bed from her and said, "Poor old Pepsi. You must miss him so much".

Kim was taken aback "How did you know his name?" she asked. Janu replied, that Kim must have mentioned the dog earlier. Kim wasn't convinced, as she still found talking about him very painful.

The two women and the dog then went upstairs. Kim then showed Janu into her daughter Nicola's room. The room had a double bed, built in wardrobes and a set of bookshelves complete with soft toys. How Kim wished it was her daughter that was there with her and not this strange character! She left them, closed the door and went to her own room. Once inside she sat on the bed ate her sandwich and drank her soup. I really should brush my teeth. "Ah to hell with tooth decay!" she thought. Once under the quilt she planned what she would do in the morning, which was only a few hours away as it was already 4a.m. She set the alarm clock for eight o'clock. Normally she would wake up at 7.15. her usual time to get up, but after having a mammoth sleep earlier and considering the time now, she didn't trust herself to waken on time. She switched off the bedside light and was just beginning to drift off to sleep, when she heard muffled voices. She lay straining her ears, a woman's voice, obviously Janu's and there was also another much deeper voice.

"A talking dog? I'm losing my mind", she thought. She got out of bed and went to open her bedroom door. No sooner had she turned the door handle, when the voices abruptly stopped. Kim stood for a few minutes wondering what she should do. There was no way she could drive anywhere because of the snow. If she were to phone anyone at this time in the morning, telling them she had a crazy woman with a talking dog in her home, it would be a one-way ticket to the funny farm. Kim had no option but to go back to bed: she would deal with her visitors in the morning.

Kim opened her eyes to a perfect blue sky with wispy clouds overhead. She was sitting on a deck chair; the old fashioned type with the canvas seat. Beside her Tom was sipping a cold beer. They were on board a beautiful, gleaming, white yacht, its sails billowing in a slight breeze. She couldn't remember being so happy. Tom lent over to kiss her. At that moment there was a loud crack of thunder, the sky turned black and in an instant a violent storm was raging all around them. Gigantic waves were crashing onto the deck. Kim watched in horror as one swept Tom overboard. She stood on the deck helpless as the waves carried him further and further away.

CHAPTER 9

THE NIGHTMARE BEGINS

B eep, beep, beep came a familiar sound in the distance. Slowly Kim awoke. Just another bad dream: nightmares had become a regular occurrence since Tom had left. As she lay in bed becoming fully awake, she began to hope the woman and her dog were also a bad dream. Gemini barking on the landing confirmed it had not been a dream. Wearily she began to get dressed; a plan of action was what was needed. First, check the weather conditions. She looked out the window- great no more snow. If she couldn't get the jeep out, she would phone her nearest neighbour, a farmer who lived about two miles away. He could get his tractor through anything. She would ask him to take Janu into town, where her boyfriend could collect her and then Kim could get back to some kind of normality. Feeling positive, she opened the bedroom door. On seeing Kim, Gemini padded downstairs. As Kim passed her daughter's bedroom she noticed the curtains were still drawn. As she entered the room she found the wardrobe door was open. The bed was made up and there was no sign of Janu. She opened the curtains and then as she tried to close the wardrobe, the door jammed on something lying on the floor. She opened it again to remove the obstruction and was amazed to find all of Nicola's lovely clothes lying discarded in a heap. Her amazement turned to anger on seeing Janu's clothes replacing them on the hangers.

Kim could feel rage building up inside her as she stooped to pick up Nicola's clothes.

"How dare she dump *my* daughter's clothes on the floor of *my* house and hang up what appeared to be mostly washed out rags from charity shops!". Trying to control her anger, she stomped down stairs. Halfway down she was stopped by a blood-curdling howl. She had heard many dogs cry in pain, whether it be due to injury or some painful illness. She had never heard any dog howl like this before. The sound was coming from the kitchen. She rushed down the stairs and pushed the door open. She found Janu kneeling on the floor beside Gemini, who had collapsed howling on the floor. He was on his side, shaking violently. Janu pleaded hysterically with Kim to "Do something!" Kim's mind was racing, what on earth could be wrong. She had heard of dogs having heart attacks, although she'd never witnessed any. It could be any one of a thousand reasons. She ran to the sitting room to phone the vet. Lifting the receiver she was devastated to find the line completely dead. "Great" she said aloud. This was not an unusual occurrence the phone line ran down her drive and then across the road through a wooded area. Sometimes after heavy snow, trees would come down bringing the phone lines down with them. Kim had no choice. She would have to drive the dog into the vets. She grabbed a throw from the back of the couch and rushed back to the kitchen. Gemini's condition hadn't altered much although he was yelping more than howling. She handed the throw to Janu, saying "Wrap him in this, I'll start the car". Grabbing her bag and car keys, she dashed to the front door. On opening the door, it was evident that Janu must have been out earlier. There were clear tracks in the deep snow heading towards the jeep. Janu must have left something in the jeep and gone to retrieve it this morning, thought Kim briefly. Climbing into the jeep she put the key into the ignition and checked to make sure the gear was in neutral: the last thing she needed right now was to stall. She turned the key. Nothing happened. Kim thumped her hands on the steering wheel in frustration. "Calm down!" she told herself. She tried again and again the only sound was the click of the key in the ignition. She thought about lifting the bonnet to have a look, but there was no point in that as she knew jack shit about the mechanics of a car. Getting out of the jeep, she kicked the tyre and cursed. "What the hell was she going to do now?" Looking up, she saw Janu standing in the doorway holding Gemini, who appeared to be much calmer. As Kim approached them, Janu explained the dog had suffered similar attacks in the past and usually after a day or two's rest, he made a complete recovery.

Once back inside, Kim lit the fire while Janu fussed over the little dog. Whilst lighting the fire, Kim's mind was racing as to what to do next. She had no phone, no transport and a nutcase with a sick dog. There was also the episode with the wardrobe. She still wanted to confront Janu, but felt in her present mental state the woman might just flip. To get some space, Kim went into the kitchen, glancing at the wall clock as she entered. It said – 9.15 a.m, so she had been up for over an hour without her usual caffeine injection. Normally, by this time she would have consumed at least three mugs of strong, black coffee to kick-start her day. Switching the kettle on, she thought, "At least I've still got electricity!" It wouldn't be the first time the power lines had come down with heavy snow. "Ah the joys of country living", she thought, leaning on the worktop and looking out at her garden, which still contained plenty of winter vegetables parsnips, brussel sprouts, leeks, carrots and turnips. "Well at least I won't starve", she thought, staring out of the window and remembering the evening at Elysium.

CHAPTER 10

THE ROMANTIC WEEKEND

Once inside the room, Sonnetta left Kim surveying her surroundings. The bed, if you could call it that, was a wooden construction, no more than 6 inches off the floor, with a foam mattress. Folded at the bottom of the bed, were a couple of blankets. The only other item of furniture was a white plastic chair, the type used as garden seats. Kim began to cry. Turning to Tom, she said, "Is this what you call a romantic weekend?"

To her amazement, instead of apologising for the cock-up, he turned on her; saying she was snobbish, boring and obviously unwilling to try something new and unconventional. He refused to leave, at least until the morning. After his unprovoked tirade, he stormed out. Kim sank down onto the mattress, buried her face into Pepsi's neck and sobbed.

Half an hour later Tom returned. Kim didn't look up; she just sat there stroking the dog. Tom had completely changed his attitude. He came over and sat down beside her. He begged her to forgive him, saying, they would leave first thing in the morning. He told her he didn't know what had come over him and that he must have got carried away with the old boy. He assured her he had now come to his senses. Kim softened, she told herself, nobody is perfect, everyone makes mistakes and Tom could be quite gullible at times.

At seven thirty they made their way to the dining room. There must have been around thirty people in the room. Trestle tables were laid out with a buffet style meal. There were no tables and chairs, so most people sat on the floor. At the end of one of the buffet tables was a pile of assorted plates. The first two plates Kim picked up were chipped. She settled for the third, which was actually a soup plate. Now for the banquet! You could have a choice of beans, lentils, beans and lentils or lentils and beans. If this was their normal diet they'd be able to have their own methane gas station! That would solve their energy problem, as there was no electricity.

CHAPTER 11

THE RUGBY SHIRT

As Kim stared out of her kitchen window, the snow began to fall again. The sky was growing darker "Oh no, not more snow," she groaned. After making herself a strong cup of coffee, she sat at the table." If only Tom were here now he'd know what to do", she thought. Not even Tom would turn out a sick dog and a fruitcake. Finishing her coffee, she went to make a second cup. As she poured her coffee, a strange chanting sound could be heard coming from the sitting room. Perhaps the little dog had died and Janu was performing some ritual. Well, if the dog is dead, she thought callously, she wouldn't have to put up with Janu any longer. Even if Kim had to walk the two miles to the neighbouring farm, it would be worth it to rid herself of Janu.

As she entered the sitting room, Gemini tried to stand; he held up his hind leg and seemed to be in a great deal of pain. Kim asked Janu if she'd mind if she examined the dog. Janu declined Kim's request, explaining that an expert had already diagnosed the dog. He had a rare genetic condition called selabrocsis and usually after a couple of days he would be back to normal. In the meantime, he must be kept warm and quiet with no stress. Kim had never heard of this condition, but after all, she wasn't a vet, and there must be hundreds, if not thousands of diseases. Kim desperately wanted to confront Janu about the clothes in the wardrobe. She couldn't trust herself not to blow a fuse, so instead she excused herself saying she'd make some soup for lunch.

As Kim was rummaging in the fridge for some vegetables, Janu approached her saying Gemini was asleep. Suddenly Janu threw her arms around Kim, holding on to her so tightly she could hardly breathe. Janu was sobbing, again and again. She thanked Kim for the kindness she'd shown her and Gemini. Kim felt really uncomfortable. She repeatedly told Janu it was okay, until eventually Janu released her from her embrace. Janu then turned to Kim saying "You look exhausted, go and sit by the fire while I make you a coffee". Kim began to protest, then decided she didn't have the energy to argue.

Kim flopped into the chair beside the fire. She felt totally drained and the events of the last 24 hours had zapped what little reserves she had. Gemini lay on a blanket in front of the fire. As she studied the dog, she thought one of its hind legs looked swollen. Gently she felt his leg; it was definitely swollen and hot to the touch. The swelling was consistent with a trauma. "How could the dog injure himself in the house? Had fallen downstairs perhaps?" The dog had been in the kitchen with Janu when it happened. The hair on the back of

Kim's neck stood up and she visibly shivered. "Had Janu sensed that Kim was coming downstairs to read the riot act? Had she deliberately injured her own dog, to avoid a confrontation?". Kim again examined the leg, this time she gently parted the hair. Being a white dog often the skin pigment was pink, if this was the case with Gemini, it would be easy to spot bruising. Sure enough he had pink skin, which showed definite discolouration due to bruising. Kim felt sick; how could anyone do something like that especially to her own animal?

She looked up. Janu stood in the doorway. "Had she seen her examine the dog? Did she know what Kim suspected?". Kim tried to appear calm and friendly, not wanting to arouse any suspicion. Janu handed Kim her coffee and then sat opposite her on the sofa. Kim sipped at her coffee. It was strong and black just the way she liked it. Janu sat on the floor stroking the dog and humming softly. It must have been the morning's events, combined with her broken sleep the previous night, but Kim suddenly felt drained and slumped back into the chair.

Kim awoke slowly. There was a beautiful aroma of cooking in the air and Janu could be heard humming in the kitchen. The room was lit only by the glow of the fire; the dog still lay on the blanket. Looking at her watch she saw it was 5.30 p.m. According to her estimations she had slept for about seven hours. Kim thought about the events of the last 24 hours. Twice she had fallen into long, deep sleeps, both times after drinking something prepared by Janu. Could this nutcase be drugging her and if so why? Kim couldn't remember ever being so afraid. She began to piece together the last 24 hours. This was becoming like a Steven King novel. "If Janu was drugging her then why hadn't the second cup of tea Janu had given her had any affect? Of course!". Kim realized, "I spilled it". That would also explain the look of annoyance on Janu's face at the time.

Janu entered the room; Kim closed her eyes pretending to be asleep. She needed more time to formulate a plan, to get herself out of this intolerable situation. Janu put a couple of logs on the fire. She then knelt beside Gemini, stroking him and whispering something over and over again. Kim listened intently trying to make out what she was saying. It sounded like "for it's me, for it's me". "No that wasn't it". To her horror, she realised Janu was saying; "Forgive me". Kim's suspicions had been correct; the evil bitch had injured her own dog. "Probably a kick", Kim thought. If she could do that to Gemini, what else was she capable of? Almost as if Janu was reading her mind, she stopped and approached Kim who remained perfectly still, frozen in fear for what seemed like an eternity. Janu was so close, Kim could feel her breath against her face. Eventually Janu left the room and went upstairs.

Kim decided from now on. She would not to eat or drink anything Janu gave her. Once her head cleared she would come up with a plan to get the hell out of here. A more pressing problem was a full bladder. Kim sat up and switched on the lamp beside her, Gemini stirred, kneeling beside him she felt his leg; it was badly swollen and very hot. As Kim stroked the little dog's head, he looked at her, his eyes no longer piercing, but pleading. For the first time since arriving, he began to wag his tail. "Poor little thing!" she thought. If at all possible, she would take him with her when she escaped, as God knows what the crazy woman might do to him if she didn't.

Kim heard footsteps coming downstairs. Janu entered the sitting room. "Feeling better?" she said. Kim stared in disbelief at what Janu was wearing; it was her son Adam's rugby shirt. There was no mistaking it as his nickname and school badge were printed on the front. She felt herself take a step back and almost fell onto the couch. Janu rushed forward catching hold of her "Are you okay?" she said. Kim explained, she felt a little queasy and needed to use the toilet. Janu insisted on coming with her in case she fainted, and began to lead Kim upstairs to the bathroom. Kim allowed herself to be supported as her legs felt like jelly and her head was beginning to pound. "Oh please not a migraine!", she thought. Kim had suffered from this terrible affliction since puberty. She had tried changing her diet to see if any foods were the trigger but to no avail and Tom had suggested trying herbal remedies. " Was that after he'd got in tow with the hippies?", she wondered.

Once inside the toilet, Kim went to close the door but Janu followed her in. "I think I can manage now" she said. Janu refused to leave and Kim couldn't wait any longer – she *had* to pee. Feeling very self-conscious, she reluctantly pulled down her trousers. Janu, meanwhile, sat casually on the edge of the bath watching her. When she had finished, they went back downstairs. As Janu guided Kim into the kitchen, she said she had prepared a special vegetarian soup and some unleavened bread. Once Kim was seated at the table, she served them both. Kim watched carefully as the soup was dished. Although she was famished, she still suspected Janu of drugging her, but why? "Why did she want to stay here with Kim? It didn't make any sense, but then nothing that had happened over the last 24 hours made sense!". Here she was, sharing a meal with this strange hippie woman and the memories of the last meal she had at Elysium came flooding back.

CHAPTER 12

THE CEREMONY

She remembered Sonnetta calling for attention after the meal that had consisted of various pulses that tasted of nothing in particular. Sonnetta announced, that as it was the summer solstice, there was going to be a special ceremony. This would take place at nine o'clock, behind the house and everyone was expected to attend. A large bonfire had been lit and already some people were standing around it. Kim had reluctantly plodded on behind Tom as they made their way towards the meeting place. There was a definite air of excitement as Garda appeared dressed in a long white robe, a wooden staff in one hand and what looked like a large crystal in the other. Sonnetta followed behind, carrying a basket filled with petals. Gorda then began a long speech about mankind's evil towards his fellow human beings and the planet. Everyone in the crowd, including Tom seemed to be hypnotised by the old man's presence.

Next he wandered among the gathered crowd. He touched one, two, three women, on their shoulders, who then followed him back to where Sonnetta was waiting. He then announced to everyone that these three women had been chosen as his disciples. As of now they would move to the top floor of the house and there he and Sonnetta would give them special training. "Special training my ass!" thought Kim. "Funny how he had picked the three most attractive women. Now can we get out of here?" Tom looked shocked, "You just don't get it do you?" he said. Kim stood in stunned silence: he'd obviously been brainwashed, just like the rest of them. "Ok" Kim thought. "I haven't much choice, I'll go along with the charade for one night, but tomorrow I'm out of here with, or without Tom!". As if he sensed her mood, Pepsi nudged her hand, Kim stroked his head. At least Pepsi didn't seem to be affected by the brainwashing.

The three women followed Sonnetta into the house. Twenty minutes later they reappeared, dressed in ankle-length, dark, green dresses. Gorda touched each one on the forehead with a crystal, at the same time chanting in what sounded like Arabic. Meanwhile, Sonnetta was sprinkling the women with petals from the basket she was carrying.

When the ceremony was finished everyone began clapping. Once the clapping subsided Sonnetta began to chant "Gorda... Gorda... Gorda". The rest of the people joined in the chant and it became louder and louder. It seemed to go on forever becoming hypnotically repetitive until it reached fever pitch. The three women seemed to be in a trance. Some people began to faint and others were lying on the ground their arms and legs thrashing the air as if they were having a fit. It was all too much for Kim; she tapped Pepsi on the head and made her way to the car. Tom was completely oblivious to her leaving. Kim caught a glimpse of him jumping up and down chanting with the others. She put Pepsi in the back seat of the car, started the engine and was gone.

CHAPTER 13

BEST EVER FRIENDS

Kim had to admit, the soup Janu had made smelled delicious. She had obviously gone out into the garden and gathered a selection of vegetables. Considering there was about eight inches of snow, this had been no easy task. The freshly made bread was also very tempting. She came to the conclusion, that if Janu was prepared to eat the food there was no way it could be drugged. They began eating. As she ate, Kim decided she would have to gain Janu's trust. She started to formulate a plan of escape, meanwhile congratulating Janu on her excellent cooking. After she had finished her meal, Kim excused herself saying she was going for a bath. Janu said she would wash-up, see to the fire and carry Gemini out for "Toilets". Kim went upstairs; she turned the bath water on, deliberately leaving the door open so that Janu would hear it running. Then she slipped quietly into Adam's room, not knowing what she would find. When she opened the door, she could not believe her eyes. The room was completely empty, no bed, no posters, no curtains, not even a carpet, everything was gone. On the floor in vivid purple paint, was a large circle, roughly six feet in diameter. Inside were lots of crudely drawn matchstick figures, people, animals, fish, birds and other weird symbols. She immediately recognised the paint as Nicola's, which she had insisted on using in her bedroom during her purple period. Then the crash of a plate breaking on the kitchen floor startled Kim. She hurried, out of the room back to the bathroom, just in time, as the bath water had almost reached the over-flow. She pulled the plug out to allow the level to drop slightly; thankfully the water was still hot. She poured in some bubble bath and locked the door.

Once in the bath Kim couldn't get the vision of Adam's room out of her mind. Janu must have cleared it while she slept, but where had she put all the furniture? Not in Nicola's room. There wasn't enough space. The only explanation she could arrive at was that Janu had carried everything downstairs, and then stored the contents of the room in the garage. There were also the strange drawings on the floor, what did they represent? Was Janu performing some kind of satanic rights? Kim shuddered. She suddenly felt chilled to the bone.

There was a tap on the door, "Teas ready!", called Janu cheerfully. "I'll be down in a minute" replied Kim. "How the hell am I going to get out of drinking the tea?", she thought. Getting out of the bath, she put on her bathrobe, then went downstairs. On seeing Kim enter the sitting room, Gemini tried to stand. The little dog struggled to his feet, but was unable to put any weight on his injured leg. As soon as he tried to take a step, he let out a howl. Kim rushed towards the dog, but was quickly overtaken by Janu who began fussing over the little dog. Kim offered to give Gemini some pain relief. She was sure she still had some anti-inflammatories left for Pepsi's arthritis. Janu refused, saying her dog would never be given chemicals, as they did more harm than good. Janu left the room, returning a short time later with two mugs of herbal tea and. handed one of the mugs to Kim. Looking quickly for somewhere to dispose of the tea, she glanced around the room. On the bookshelves beside the fire was a large pottery vase filled with pot-pouri, "perfect!" thought Kim, and sat down on the sofa beside the vase. Janu sat on the chair opposite her.

Kim pretended to sip her tea. Suddenly she had a brilliant idea. If she could convince Janu she was her friend, then maybe she would relax her vigilance. Kim could then get herself away from this psycho. Kim began by telling her how much she was enjoying the 'girlie' company, as the long, dark, winter nights were lonely and depressing. This seemed to please Janu, so Kim decided to lay it on thick. She told her it must have been fate, that she was on the road at that time the day before, as normally she would still have been at work and that the fact Janu had a dog was the icing on the cake, now that old Pepsi had gone. Watching her reaction, Kim could see her plan was working, she was grinning from ear to ear. Suddenly Janu leapt up, came over to Kim throwing her arms around her. Kim returned the hug trying to be as convincing as possible. Janu then did something completely unexpected. Taking the mug from Kim, Janu said, "Let's celebrate, we are after all, best ever friends". Astonished, Kim said, "Celebrate, how?"

Janu disappeared into the kitchen. The cuddle from Janu gave Kim the creeps. "Don't tell me she's a lesbian as well as mad!" she thought. Janu returned with a bottle of wine and two glasses. She poured the wine, handed a glass to Kim, then Janu raised her glass "To my best ever friend". Kim responded by repeating the toast, trying not to choke on the words.

The rest of the evening, the two women sat drinking wine and chatting. Kim told Janu about her work, her last dog, and her vegetable garden. She was careful not to mention anything about her children or Tom. After a few glasses of wine it became apparent that Janu was quite tipsy. She became quite giggly, almost child like, continually referring to Kim as, her best ever friend. In contrast, Kim felt little or no effect from the wine. After all it was quite normal for her to drink this amount everyday. She had done so for many years, as she and Tom had shared a bottle of wine with their evening meal every night. In fact they had shared everything together: their love of the countryside, good food, fine wines and, of course, their children. Adam and his father had been very close, just as she had been with Nicola.

CHAPTER 14

TOM'S RETURN

When Kim had come home that night from Elysium, she had expected Tom to return the next day, with his tail between his legs, full of apologies. In fact it was not until the Tuesday night that a taxi rolled up outside and in walked Tom, as if he had just returned home from work. On the other hand, Kim had been totally lost and miserable since coming back. Kim had tried to talk to him explaining how she'd felt while at Elysium and how she was feeling since he came home. Tom seemed torn between wanting to be with Kim and being a part of the Fellowship. They sat into the small hours trying to reach some sort of agreement. Kim was adamant she would never join the hippies. Eventually Tom, who was very much in love with her, said he would put it all behind him. They decided to carry on as before and to pretend it had never happened. For the first few months after Tom returned, he showered her with gifts: chocolates, flowers, all the usual things. For some time, Kim had been hinting about having a new kitchen installed. There was nothing wrong with the solid pine one they had, apart from the fact that it looked a little shabby and had been in the house as long as they had. One evening, Tom produced a glossy kitchen catalogue, telling Kim to choose whatever she liked and not to worry about the price. After browsing through, they agreed on the solid oak, with granite worktops, in keeping with the country cottage style. Once installed, it became Kim's pride and joy. She often commented that it looked like something out of the Ideal Homes Exhibition. Unfortunately, all the material acquisitions in the world would not be able to save their marriage. Her efforts to become the perfect wife, cooking special meals, taking extra care in her appearance, were of no avail. She would often find Tom deep in thought, with that far away look in his eyes and could see that he was back in Elysium. After few months the inevitable happened. At the end of October, when summer had gone and the first signs of winter were approaching. Tom left.... this time for good. He told Kim he planned to sell his business and invest the money in Elysium. Everything else, he would leave to her, including Bluebell Cottage

CHAPTER 15

THE TOAST

Kim suggested to Janu that they open another bottle of wine. She hoped Janu would agree. She thought if she got her drunk, she could slip out of the house and walk to Kevin's farm. She didn't care if it was thick snow outside. The way she was feeling at the moment, she would walk over hot coals to get away from Janu. Unfortunately, Janu was having none of it. She was full of guilt at having fallen by the wayside, drinking the wine earlier. Kim had a brain wave; she explained to Janu when a new friendship was formed, it was a tradition in Scotland, that drinking whisky must seal the occasion. She told her of the special bottle of malt she kept under the stairs for just such an occasion. She also said if they didn't perform this ceremony, it would cause their friendship to cease. Just as she suspected, the superstitious claptrap worked, Janu agreed they must indeed carryout the tradition.

In truth, neither Kim nor indeed Tom ever drank whisky; they kept a bottle purely for the sake of offering it to their guests. Kim rose. Before going to get the whisky, she drew back the curtains. No more snow had fallen; in fact the sky was clear. It was a beautiful, clear, starry night and the snow glistened with frost. The temperature outside had plummeted, " I'd better wrap up, if I get out of here tonight" she thought. Janu, who was standing beside Kim, said excitedly "We can build a snowman tomorrow". Kim agreed, trying to sound enthusiastic. Kim asked Janu to fetch two glasses from the kitchen, while she went to get the whisky.

Kim opened the cupboard door under the stairs, which was full of the usual junk. There were golf clubs, old magazines, outdoor boots and jackets plus numerous cardboard boxes. As she pulled out one of the boxes, she found it contained an assortment of Nicola's belongings. She rummaged quickly through the box. It contained hair staighteners, a personal C.D player and old school books and Kim couldn't believe her eyes as she noticed a number of discarded mobile phones. There were four phones in all and two chargers. "I've got the glasses", said Janu standing in the doorway. Kim quickly kicked the box under a shelf. Seeing the whisky beside the picnic hamper; she grabbed it and came out of the cupboard. "Ah here we are" she said holding up the bottle. She could hardly contain her excitement at finding the phones, at the same time feeling rather stupid at not having one of her own. After Tom left, both Nicola and Adam had insisted she get a mobile. It was one of these things she had been meaning to do, but had never got around to. When Tom was here he had a mobile phone so she'd never needed one. Tom wouldn't go anywhere without it, he even took it into the bathroom. Kim sometimes thought there was an invisible umbilical cord between him and that phone.

Kim poured two large whiskies into the glasses. "You must make a Scottish toast!" said Janu. Kim raised her glass, "clach na brea dras lach!" they clinked their glasses together. Kim told Janu she must drink the contents of the glass in one go. They both finished their drinks. Janu asked Kim to translate what she had just said, Kim told her roughly translated, it meant they would be friends till the moon fell from the sky. This of course was utter crap, as she didn't know a single word of Gaelic. Janu swallowed the translation as well as the whisky. Both women sat on the sofa. Kim felt slightly intoxicated: Janu on the other hand was beginning to slur her speech and was obviously pretty drunk. Kim decided to wait five more minutes until Janu became drowsier, before going to bed. Hopefully once in bed she would go into a deep sleep. This would give Kim a better chance of escape.

Sitting there, Kim began to plan her get- away. Her wax jacket hung on the back door and her Wellies on the floor beside it. In her bedside cabinet she kept a little torch in case of power cuts. She looked down at Gemini. "what was she going to do about the dog?". She was afraid to leave him for fear that Janu would take her rage out on him, once she discovered Kim had gone. After all, hadn't she kicked the dog earlier that day? Kim was convinced she had. There was nothing else for it; she'd have to carry him. Concerned the dog might howl when she picked him up, Kim decided she'd have to give him a painkiller. She would have to find a way of giving him a pill before she went to bed. She only hoped that Janu would leave him downstairs tonight.

Kim made an excuse to go to the kitchen for a glass of milk for them both, saying it would help to dilute the alcohol. While she was in the kitchen, she unwrapped one of Pepsi's pills and hid it in a piece of gammon. She prayed that the dog wouldn't spit it out and give the game away. Returning to the sitting room, she handed Janu the milk; "I thought since we've been indulging ourselves tonight, Gemini could get a little treat too" said Kim. Janu looked at the piece of meat that Kim was holding and nodded her drunken head. Here goes, thought Kim, please God don't let him spit out the pill. Half a tablet would have been enough for such a small dog but she decided it would be better to give him a stronger dose. After all, the worst thing that could happen would be that the little dog would become drowsy. She offered Gemini the meat and he sniffed it cautiously. Then, as if he knew that she was trying to help him, he gently took it out of her hand and swallowed it whole. Kim let out a sigh of relief.

The effects of alcohol had been working on Janu, who was not paying attention and beginning to drift off. "I think we should go to bed" said Kim, Janu opened her tired eyes and nodded, "What about Gemini?" she enquired. "Well if you want my professional opinion" said Kim, "He shouldn't be moved". This seemed to satisfy Janu who began to stumble up the stairs to bed. As if it were a regular day, both women used the bathroom and got ready for bed. Kim said goodnight to

Janu on the landing and in return, Janu embraced Kim, telling her that she had never been happier in all her life. Janu leaned in closer as if to kiss Kim, startled Kim pulled back, pretending to stagger. Janu began to laugh; believing Kim to be drunk then turned and went to her room. Kim switched off the landing light and went to her own room, closing the door loudly. Once inside, Kim quietly but hastily, changed into her warmest night dress and carefully opened the bedside cabinet drawer to get out the small torch. She checked the batteries- fine. Glancing at the alarm clock she noticed it was ten after midnight. Creeping to the bedroom door she opened it slightly.

CHAPTER 16

ESCAPE

She lay on top of the bed, afraid to snuggle up under the warm duvet, in case she should fall asleep. She would wait an hour, long enough to make sure that Janu was deeply asleep. There was no doubt that the alcohol was having an effect on Kim and she could feel herself becoming drowsy. She decided to sit upright; perhaps this would make it easier to stay awake. She arranged the pillows against the headboard and sat up. Only ten minutes had passed and already she was beginning to feel cold. The only good thing about feeling cold was that she no longer felt sleepy. Where had the torch gone? Hadn't she put it on the bed? In a panic, she began feeling around the bed. After what felt like an age, her fingers touched the cold plastic of the torch, which had rolled under the cover. She grabbed it and lay back against the headboard. It was a solid pine headboard that Tom and Kim had bought together, the memory felt like another life. Tom had always taken pride in the house and unlike many men he took an active interest in the interior décor. The bed had been bought soon after Tom had come back from Elysium.

They had decided to give the house a makeover, as if by doing so it would bring a new lease of life into the marriage. Of course it didn't work.

Kim often went on days out with Tom, if he was working on a new development or travelling to an area that she had never been. She had been as far north as Kirkwall, as far south as Kelso and covered and most of the east and west coasts. Unfortunately, when Tom had gone to Elysium to value the house and grounds, which was formerly called Blair House, Kim was in bed with flu. She had planned to go with him as he had shown her the plans and they had even discussed buying the house themselves. Tom knew that it would need a lot of money spent on it to bring it to a decent standard but he felt it would be a challenging investment, which would pay off. They even talked about Kim running it as a country house hotel. He set off early in the morning to view the property. When he came back he told Kim that it was in much worse condition than he envisaged. Instead of buying the property, Tom would advertise it, although he did not hold out much hope for a quick sale. That was in February last year, but to his surprise it had been on the market less than a week when he received an offer considerably above the asking price. Tom contacted the owners who accepted the offer immediately. As far as Kim knew, that was the last contact he had had with the house or the new owners. How wrong she had been.

Kim woke shivering. "Shit", she thought, "I must have dozed off". She looked at the alarm clock, which read 3:20am. She sat upright, straining her ears but the house was completely silent. She carefully slid her legs over the side of the bed and slowly stood up. She could feel the beginnings of a dull headache, the kind triggered by alcohol and her mouth felt furry with dryness. Shivering, both with the cold and with nerves, she slipped a jumper over her nightdress and struggled to pull on a pair of jeans. She fumbled on the floor for a few seconds until she found a pair of socks and then she went to the doorway. She decided not to chance putting on the torch until she was outside. She knew the layout of the house well enough to move around easily in the dark. Once on the landing she paused outside Janu's room, then pressing her ear against the tiny gap between the door and the doorframe, she listened. She could hear the faint sound of regular, deep breathing. Silently she crept downstairs, her heart beating so loudly that she thought Janu would clearly hear it. "Don't be stupid" she thought, "Calm down".

Once downstairs, she went into the kitchen for her thick padded jacket, which was hanging behind the door next to her wellies. She pulled them both on and returned to the hallway. At the foot of the stairs she again paused and listened for movement at janu's room. Again there was nothing but silence. "So far so good" she thought. Now she would open the front door before picking up Gemini. That way she wouldn't be trying to hold on to the dog while struggling to open the door. Slowly she approached the door, feeling along the wall as she went. At last she touched the door and felt for the handle. She turned it slowly and gently, then pulled it. Nothing happened. It didn't move. Kim always left the keys in the keyhole as she had lost count of the times that she and Tom would be ready to leave only to discover that they could not find the keys. So they decided that they would get into the habit of leaving the keys in the lock and for as long as Kim could remember, that was where the keys were kept. She slid her hand down to the keyhole. It was empty. She felt tears of frustration well up in her eyes. She was close to screaming. "Stay calm" she told herself. Okay it had been more difficult than she had first thought, but she would just have to leave by the back door. She headed to the kitchen, stopping again at the bottom of the stairs. There was still no sound. She crept back to the kitchen, feeling her way around the table to the back door. The back door key was in Kim's handbag, which she had left in the car that morning so there was no way that Janu could have locked this door as well. Feeling quite confident again, Kim slowly turned the doorknob and again gently pulled. Once again she met resistance. "No!" she said audibly and before she good help herself. Kim began to sob, she felt crushed. At that moment she heard the bedroom door open and the landing light click on. Panic over took her for a few seconds. "What would she do?". She stood frozen as she listened to Janu walking towards the bathroom door. She paused, then changed direction and began descending the staircase.

CHAPTER 17

ADAM AND NICOLA

Forty miles away Adam was blissfully unaware of his mother's predicament. He was a first year university student studying law. He had excelled at school and was a gifted sportsman. Rugby was his sport of choice although he also played tennis, golf and was an accomplished skier. About six foot tall, with a muscular physique, flawless skin and dark hair. Perhaps because of all these attributes, as well as an outgoing personality, he was a popular choice with the opposite sex. Adam was enjoying his first year at University, enjoying the vibrancy and excitement of the city, a stark contrast to the isolation of Bluebell Cottage. As a child, Bluebell Cottage had been fun but as he reached the age of 15 or 16, he wanted to spend more time in the town with his friends, socialising and competing in his favourite sports. His mother mainly had the unenviable task of being his personal chauffer as a teenager but at the age of 17, he sat his driving test and true to form, passed first time. As a reward Tom bought his son a Ford Fiesta.

At the same time that his mother was creeping around downstairs in Bluebell Cottage, Adam was creeping upstairs with his latest conquest. She was also a first year student, staying in the halls of residence. Adam was fortunate to have his own flat, which his parents had bought. Tom had decided it would be an investment property, and in 4 years time, when Adam graduated, he would sell it on or rent it out. The only drawback to the flat was that it was some distance from the city centre. Tom had always assumed that Adam would carry on in his footsteps, becoming first a partner in the business and eventually taking it over completely. He certainly had both the academic skills as well as the personality.

Poor Nicola on the other hand had struggled through school. She was not nearly so successful either academically or socially. She managed to get a couple of Highers and a few Standard Grades but none with good grades. Visually, she was very different to her younger brother. Around 5ft4, she had mousy brown hair, a pale complexion and constantly had to watch what she ate. Equally, the siblings differed in nature, as Nicola was shy and lacked confidence. However, unlike Adam, who could at times be arrogant and self -centred, Nicola was a very kind, selfless person. She would help anyone in any way she could. Unfortunately, a few of her friends tended to take advantage of this. Kim in particular, felt protective of her daughter. They had a special bond that only a mother and daughter can have. Of course she loved Adam dearly, but although he was 2 years younger than Nicola, was far more independent and capable.

Nicola had never wanted to go to university. She was going into nursing, a calling she had had since she was a young child. She started nursing college when she was 18 years old and after only 3 months of being away from home, she had met the boy of her dreams. Jake was from New Zealand, 25 years old and a mechanic. They had met, of all places in Tesco supermarket, after crashing their trollies. They got chatting and had a coffee together and from then on had been dating. Kim had met Jake a few times before she announced that she was heading to New Zealand to begin a new life together.

Kim had liked Jake; he was polite, quiet and was obviously very much in love with her daughter. He was constantly praising her and showering her with compliments. Jake came from the North Island. His father owned a garage there and Jake helped him run the business. He had come to Scotland for a holiday and to visit his aunt. In fact he had only been in the country for a few days before meeting Nicola. Jake hoped that she would fall in love with his homeland and want to stay. Tom and Kim however, although delighted for their daughter, hoped that she and Jake would want to settle in Scotland.

CHAPTER 18

BETTER NOW

Kim only had a few seconds to react. She pulled off the jacket and hung it behind the door. With lightening speed, she removed her wellies, throwing them on the floor. Lastly, pulling off her jeans and jumper, she quickly scanned the kitchen for somewhere to hide them and decided on the washing machine. She had no sooner put them in and closed the door when Janu clicked on the kitchen light. She stood staring at Kim. Kim couldn't decide whether the look on her face was anger, surprise or suspicion. She guessed, probably all three.

Kim began to tremble; she could feel her stomach turn and knew she was going to throw up. She looked at the sink, it was too far away. Beside her, was a bucket and mop, just in time Kim dropped to her knees and was immediately sick. Janu's expression changed to concern at seeing Kim retching violently and shaking from head to toe. Janu dashed over to the sink and grabbed a tea towel soaked in water. She knelt beside Kim and held the cloth to her forehead all the time stroking her hair and asking if she were all right. Eventually Kim stopped retching and slumped back. Janu helped her to her feet and sat her at the kitchen table. She wrapped her arms around Kim's shoulders. She then went to the sink and poured a glass of water, which she gave to Kim to sip. Kim was sobbing. Janu gently wiped her face with the wet cloth and then patted it dry with a towel. Next she boiled the kettle and filled a hot water bottle and then helped Kim upstairs to her bedroom. She pulled back the duvet and helped her into bed. "Better now?" Janu said. Kim could only nod. She was devastated that she was back to square one. Janu switched out the light on the landing, but instead of going back to her own room, she insisted on joining Kim, snuggling up beside her.

CHAPTER 19

THE YURT

Tom's first few weeks at Elysium flew past. He was allocated a living space in one of the yurts, which he shared with Alex and the three children. Alex's wife was one of the three women that Gorda had chosen to be his disciples. The yurt was a circular dwelling, of the type used by Mongolians. Inside was pretty basic. They all slept on mattresses on the floor that doubled as seats during the day. Heating was provided by a wood-burning stove, which was also used as a rudimentary cooker.

His days along with the rest of the adults were filled with clearing and digging an area that would later be used as a vegetable plot and also collecting firewood. He found the manual work demanding having worked in a nine to five, office job all his life. In the evenings he would often go to the house to listen to Gorda's sermons. Sonnetta and the other three women would usually sit beside Gorda, respectfully staring ahead. Only Sonnetta would occasionally speak at such meetings.

Some of the group, which by now numbered fifty, had begun to replace the boarded windows. The interiors had been cleaned and freshly painted. Tom wondered how Alex felt about his wife being segregated from him and her children. After all, Tom had freely chosen to leave his wife, but this was not the case for Alex. Although Alex never complained, the three children aged between twelve and four missed their mother, especially Becky the youngest. Tom and Alex became like an odd couple, sharing the parenting between them. At the beginning of December a new member arrived at Elysium and it was decided that she would join Alex, Tom and the children in their yurt. It was hoped that a female presence would restore balance, thus helping the children, especially Becky to adjust to her mother's absence. She had begun to have tantrums as well as bed-wetting.

CHAPTER 20

GINA

Gina was a young attractive woman probably in her mid thirties. She was easy going and had a natural ability with the children, who had taken a shine to her instantly. Gina suggested Becky, the youngest child, sleep with her to give her extra security. After only a week the bed-wetting and tantrums had almost stopped. As it was the winter, Tom and the rest of his little unit (as that is what each small group was called) spent a good deal of time together. Tom and Gina got along really well; they could sit for hours discussing anything from politics to what they would make for dinner.

CHAPTER 21

THE FEVER

Over the next few days, Kim's fever worsened, on occasions her temperature soared and she would be soaked in sweat. Janu would sponge her down; change her nightie and the bed linen, to try to make her comfortable again. At other times she would be shivering and chilled to the bone. During these episodes Janu would snuggle in beside her to keep her warm. She nursed Kim diligently for three days, bringing soup and drinks to make sure she did not become dehydrated. Kim knew she had a touch of pneumonia. The night lying on top of the bed in her already fragile state had left her vulnerable and open to infection. During those three days of fever, Kim was only vaguely aware of what was happening. She would be lucid some of the time. During one of these spells, she lay trying to recollect what had happened in the previous days. She could remember picking up Janu and the terrible realisation that she had been drugged. The bitter disappointment she had experienced after her attempted escape failed so miserably.

It was while she lay contemplating what to do next that she thought she heard the phone ringing. It only rang perhaps once or twice before it stopped. She could hear Janu's muffled voice speaking briefly and then silence. After a few seconds the sound of footsteps could be heard coming up the stairs. The footsteps came to halt outside the bedroom door. Slowly the door handle turned and the door opened. Kim closed her eyes and pretended to be asleep. Janu approached the bed. She stooped, her head only inches from Kim's face. Kim lay perfectly still, breathing heavily. After what seemed like an eternity, Janu slowly left the room and descended the stairs.

"Plan B" thought Kim. She was sure there was no way she could use the phone in the sitting room, without Janu finding out: if indeed it was still working. Had she imagined she heard it ringing? It was then, she remembered Nicola's phone box under the stairs. There had been at least two chargers and about four mobiles the last time she looked. "Surely she would get one of the phones and chargers to work? First things first, she would have to regain her strength."

For the next two days she tried to sleep, eat and drink as much as possible. On Friday morning, exactly a week since the fateful day she had picked up Janu, Kim felt strong enough to get up out of bed. She ate breakfast in bed, before announcing to Janu that she would like to go downstairs. Throughout her illness, she had not seen hide nor hair of Gemini. As she entered the sitting room she was given the welcome of a long lost friend, as the little dog danced around her feet with his tail wagging. He seemed a lot better, although he still limped quite badly.

Kim made her way to the kitchen for a glass of water. As she went through the door, she was stopped in her tracks and her eyes widened at the scene before her. Janu had been very busy during her absence. The beautiful solid oak kitchen, that Tom had painstakingly installed, had been trashed. Every cupboard door had been removed and the beautiful granite worktops that she used to be so proud of had been attacked with what must have been a chisel. Deep lines had been gouged out: crude carvings of matchstick figures, half moons, stars, flowers and other shapes she didn't recognise. Kim knew she mustn't let Janu see her reaction, for fear of reprisals. Somehow, she managed to pour a glass of water and return to the sitting room. If only Tom were here, she thought, feeling completely helpless and alone.

CHAPTER 22

BECKY

Tom in fact, had been having his own problems. In the beginning, when Gina had first arrived in the yurt, things had been good. They had quickly become close friends, enjoying each others company immensely. As far as Tom was concerned, they were simply friends. One morning after a night of particularly heavy rain, Gina had complained of a leak in the tent above, resulting in her bed becoming soaked. She insisted the bed be relocated until the leak was repaired and the floor beneath it, dried out. Instead of moving the mattress beside the other children, she placed it beside Tom's. Tom felt uncomfortable about the new sleeping arrangement, but rather than hurt Gina's feelings, he decided to let it pass for the time being. Tom, Gina and little Becky became almost like a family. Becky was like a fragile china doll. She had long black hair, a pale complexion and was very petite, just like her mother. The three of them would spend hours in the evenings, inventing games to while away the long dark nights. When they went to bed, Becky would snuggle in between Tom and Gina. After the child fell asleep one night, Tom began to tell her about his decision to join the fellowship. He told her about Kim and his family, their beautiful little cottage in the country and how he hoped she would reconsider and decide to join him.

Chapter 23

Kevin and Anna

Kevin MacLeod had farming in his genes. He had been born in Cannabrae Farm and lived and worked there all his life. He had been heard to say, the only time he would leave the house, would be when they carried him out in his coffin. It was mostly arable land, although they had a small herd of beef cattle. His family had farmed there for three generations. He had been an only child, who, it had always been understood, would work on the farm and eventually take over, when his father felt it was time to relinquish the reins.

When Kevin was twenty-three, he married his childhood sweetheart, Anna. Anna's father was the local gamekeeper: a proud man called Jock Stuart, who had reputation for being very hard on anyone he considered to be poaching. After Anna had left school, she had trained to be a dental nurse. She married Kevin shortly after her twenty-first birthday. This came as no surprise to anyone, as the two of them had been inseparable since before they left high school. Kevin's parents lived in the main farmhouse. The newly-weds moved in to the farm cottage, which in years gone by, had always been for the farm workers. The cottage was about half a mile from the main farmhouse. Kevin and Anna made the perfect couple. They planned to start a family immediately.

Unfortunately, after trying unsuccessfully for three years, there was no pregnancy. Anna decided to go for tests, to find out if there was any medical reason to explain why she had not conceived. The test results were clear; there was nothing physically wrong with her. After much persuasion and cajoling, Anna finally managed to talk Kevin into going to get checked. He too was given the all clear and the two of them were told to be patient. Almost two years later, Anna finally fell pregnant. They were overjoyed, as were both sets of parents. Kevin's parents decided it was time the young couple moved in to the farmhouse. Anna quit her job and they both began to get the house ready for the new arrival. The baby was due in early June. No expense was spared and when it was finished, it was fit for a prince or princess.

About four months in to the pregnancy, Anna began to feel unwell. After a visit to the doctor she was advised to rest more. Kevin insisted she stayed in bed for a few days. On the second day she began to bleed and the doctor arranged for her to be taken to hospital immediately. By the time they arrived at the hospital, the bleeding had increased and Anna was having severe abdominal pains. Later that evening, she miscarried. They were both devastated, especially Anna. The doctors assured the couple, that women often lose their first pregnancy. They were also told; there was no reason why they should not try again. The following day Kevin collected Anna, to take her home. It was the end of January. Neither of them spoke as they made their way back to the farm. The day matched their mood; it was pouring with rain and blowing a gale. As soon as they got home, Anna went straight to bed. After few days Anna regained her strength. The two of them tried to put the episode behind them; after all, there was no reason why they couldn't try again.

In September, Anna once again fell pregnant. Everyone was overjoyed; surely this time she would carry the baby full term. Anna was wrapped in cotton wool for the next six months. Neither Kevin nor their parents would allow her to do anything they considered was too strenuous. She wasn't even allowed to lift a shopping bag. Then disaster struck. Yet again as before, she began bleeding. Kevin rushed her into hospital but unfortunately, she lost the baby. This was to happen on two more occasions and by the time Anna was thirty-five, she'd had four miscarriages. She and Kevin were still desperate for a family, but after the last miscarriage, she haemorrhaged and they were advised not to try again. Anna began to get very depressed. When Kevin came in from working, he would often find her sitting, crying in the nursery. On one of these occasions, he suggested adoption. Anna considered for several minutes before agreeing that maybe that would be the answer. They decided to make some enquiries the following day. The adoption procedure was lengthy and because they wanted a baby, were told it could take up to two years. Kevin and Anna decided they had waited this long, another two years wouldn't make much difference.

Not long after the adoption process had begun, Anna began to suffer terrible headaches. Her doctor thought it was migraine, probably triggered by the stress of her last miscarriage. She was given pain relief but the headaches increased in frequency and severity. She often had to spend days in bed. Her doctor decided to send her for a brain scan. When Anna and Kevin went to see the consultant, they were not prepared for the results. Anna was told she had a brain tumour and because of its location it was inoperable. The worst news was yet to come, the biopsy result, showed the tumour to be malignant. The best they could do was to give her radiotherapy for a few weeks. When Anna asked "How long", she was told, "Six months to a year" Anna died just before her thirty-seventh birthday.

Kevin's world collapsed, he had lost the love of his life, and he never remarried. During the next five years, he also lost his mother and father. For the last eighteen years he had ran the farm by himself. He kept very much to himself. He never had holidays, or days off. Every day was like the one before and he worked from dawn to dusk. The local people all believed he had never got over losing Anna. Once a week he would leave the farm. This was to go in to town to collect his weekly shopping.

CHAPTER 24

THE BROKEN PROMISE

After her three days in bed, Kim although on her feet, was disappointed at how weak she still felt. "I am not ready to escape just yet", she thought. Janu sat across from her, reading a book, Kim tried to make out the title. She certainly didn't recognise it from her bookshelves, which mainly contained cookery, gardening books and a few novels. Kim wondered if she should broach the subject of the phone, then decided it would be safer not to mention it. "Had she really heard the phone ringing or was it just her imagination due to her delirious state?" The sound of Janu snapping the book shut made Kim jump. Janu stood up, saying that she would "get some vegetables from the garden and make a casserole". She suggested Kim put her feet up on the couch and rest. Saying that she did indeed feel sleepy, Kim put her feet up on the couch, closed her eyes and yawned.

On hearing the back door close, she sprang into action. She tried the phone- it was still dead. Kim thought about checking to see if Janu had unplugged it, but that would mean pulling out the bookshelves to locate the socket. Deciding there wasn't enough time to do that she rushed to the cupboard under the stairs. She pulled out the box with Nicola's mobile phones, and took out the four mobiles and the two chargers. Quickly closing the door, she returned to the sitting room. She looked around the room for somewhere to hide them. 'Think!' she said to herself, beginning to panic, afraid Janu would appear at any moment. She stuffed the mobiles down the back of the settee. The chargers were not so easy to hide. Looking around the room, her eyes fell once again on the clay pot that contained the potpourri. After placing them carefully in the pot, she made sure they were completely covered.

Lying back on the settee, she could feel her heart thumping. The exertion had also caused her to become breathless. As she tried desperately to control her breathing, she suddenly felt something cold and wet against her hand. She had become so engrossed in her efforts, that she had not noticed Gemini enter the room. Kim patted the little dog, he began to lick her hand and wag his tail. She spoke softly to him, telling him she would not desert him. Just then, she heard the back door open. Gemini's tail immediately stopped wagging and curled between his legs. He turned and limped quickly back into the kitchen. Janu popped her head around the door "How are you feeling now?" she asked. Kim lied, saying that she felt weak and drowsy again, and if Janu didn't mind, she'd just snuggle up under the throw and sleep. Janu came over and began to stroke Kim's forehead. She began to sing what appeared to be a lullaby. Although Kim didn't understand any of the words, she thought they sounded Swedish, not that she could speak any foreign languages. It could have been Japanese for all she knew. Kim played along, pretending to drift off to sleep. Before she left, Janu stooped to kiss her forehead.

As soon as she was alone, Kim quickly wiped the spot where she had been kissed, shuddering with revulsion. The sound of water running confirmed Janu was in the kitchen preparing the casserole. Kim began to wonder why; after all this time, no one had missed her. OK, so she didn't have a social circle anymore, but what about her colleagues at work, surely they must be wondering where she was? It was no secret she wanted Tom back, perhaps everyone thought she had gone to Elysium, to try to save her marriage. What about the farmer, Kevin MacLeod? He passed by the end of her drive every day to feed his cattle. Surely he must have noticed there were no tyre tracks in the snow. Kim thought about it. "How could she blame him for not checking on her? Where had she been twenty years ago, when Anna was diagnosed with cancer?" Kim had just given birth to Adam and Nicola was around two years old. She had heard about the tragic events surrounding Anna and Kevin's marriage. On numerous occasions she had planned to visit Cannabrae to introduce herself. Knowing how much the couple had wanted children, the thought of going there, just after giving birth to her second child felt wrong: almost like rubbing their noses in it. So she never did visit.

Like everyone else in the neighbourhood, Tom and Kim attended the funeral. There were hundreds of mourners; the little parish church was full to capacity. Many people had to stand outside during the service. It was not only largest; it was also the most emotional funeral Tom and Kim had ever attended. Poor Kevin stood there; his grief visible to everyone. After the funeral Kim was riddled with guilt at never visiting Cannabrae before Anna's death. She made a promise to make amends by dropping in on Kevin from time to time. Of course, she never did. In fact she had never really spoken to Kevin, just the occasional "Nice day!" or "looks like rain!" if they met while she was walking the dogs. "No", she thought, "there was not much chance of Kevin driving up in his tractor to save her."

CHAPTER 25

GEMINI

In the first week in December Elysium was gripped by a severe frost. One morning after the two older children had left for their tutorials, Alex asked Gina and Tom if they would mind looking after little Becky for a short time. Once her father had gone, Becky returned to what had lately become her usual position; sitting on her mattress sucking her thumb whilst cuddling a soft toy. Recently the little girl had become withdrawn; she seldom spoke or joined in with any activities. Gina who at first had been so caring and patient now seemed almost indifferent towards her. After about an hour Alex returned. He popped his head around the door, saying he had a surprise for her. Becky did not respond. Alex opened the door fully and gave a soft whistle. A second later in trotted a little white dog, with its tail wagging furiously. On seeing the dog Becky leapt to her feet and ran over to it, throwing her arms round its neck. "What's his name?" she cried excitedly. "Gemini" replied her father. It was love at first sight and in no time at all, the little dog and Becky became inseparable. She even took him into bed with her at night. Everyone was delighted with the outcome; well not quite everyone. Gina seemed somehow displeased at all the attention being lavished on Gemini. She had tried to gain the dog's affection, by offering him titbits but he seemed nervous of her, which annoyed her intensely. After one such episode, Gina stormed out of the yurt in a rage. Taken aback, Tom and Alex looked at one another puzzled. Tom decided to follow her, to try to diffuse the situation.

Eventually he found her in one of the outbuildings and was shocked at what he saw. Gina was sitting on an old bench, tearing at her neck and arms with her fingernails. Blood trickled down her neck and arms. He had read about people self harming, but had never witnessed it or known of anyone doing it. Not quite sure how to deal with the situation, he sat down and put his arm around her. Gina threw herself into his arms sobbing. Tom tried to comfort her as best he could. When she had calmed down a little, he asked her what was wrong.

Gina began to tell him of a tragic incident that had taken place when she was a little girl. She had owned a little dog just like Gemini. One day the dog had followed her to school. On seeing the dog, her teacher had told Gina to take it home. On the way back to her house she came upon a group of teenage boys, who began teasing her. The ringleader of the group came up to her and pulled her hair. Gina began to cry and pleaded with them to let her go. In an effort to protect her, the little dog had bitten the boy on his ankle. He was outraged and signalled to one of the group to fetch a bottle out of a rucksack they had with them. While one of the gang held the little girl, the leader, poured the contents of the bottle over the dog. Then to her horror, he struck a match and set him alight. Gina said she would never forget the sight and sound, as the dog ran around in circles howling in agony, or the smell of burning flesh and hair that filled the air. She remembered screaming in terror at the horrific sight before her. This alerted a man, who on hearing the commotion, rushed out and threw his jacket over the dog to douse the flames. The gang had run off, leaving Gina. She knelt down beside her beloved dog, crying so hard she felt her heart would burst. The rescue had come too late; the little dog had taken a few gasps of air and then died in her arms.

Tom sat in stunned silence for a few minutes. Being a dog lover himself, he couldn't imagine witnessing such a terrible scene himself and it must have been far worse for a child. Tom gently wiped the tears from Gina's eyes and held her tightly. After a few minutes Gina looked up into Tom's eyes saying, "Out of all the people here in Elysium, you are my only true friend."

Over the next few weeks Tom and Gina spent more and more time together. Becky, thanks to the little dog, was once more behaving like a normal four year old. One evening, during a deep conversation Tom and Gina were having, he told her about his life before joining the fellowship. He told her about his business, his beautiful isolated cottage, Adam and Nicola who he was so proud of and finally Kim. He confided to her, how he still loved Kim and at times, felt like giving up Elysium and going back to Bluebell Cottage.

Chapter 26

The Dark

Janu entered the sitting room carrying what Kim immediately recognised as her wedding album. Sitting down opposite Kim she opened the book, taking out the first photograph, which was of Tom and Kim cutting their wedding cake. Holding the photo between both hands, Janu ripped the picture in half, throwing Kim's image into the fire. "This should have been me with Tom, not you" she cried. Outraged, Kim leapt to her feet to retrieve the book. Before Kim had the chance to snatch the album, Janu also jumped to her feet and with a sickening blow, smacked her viciously across the face with it, causing Kim to stumble backwards with the impact. Regaining her footing Kim lunged at Janu, who in turn grabbed her by the hair, pulling her head down, with such violence, that screaming in pain, she was forced to her knees. Kim's scream was cut short, when Janu cruelly brought her knee upwards, smashing it into her face. Almost unconscious, Kim was aware of blood gushing from her nose and mouth, being dragged by her hair along the floor and then pushed into the cupboard under the stairs. She was brought back to consciousness at the sound of the door closing behind her. Kim began screaming in terror at being confined in the little dark space. Janu opened the door; in her hand she held a small ornate dagger. She warned Kim if she made another sound, she'd slit her throat as easily as gutting a fish. Janu slammed the door closed. Kim once again found herself in total darkness. Sliding back along the floor on her bottom, until her back touched the wall, she curled up into the foetal position. With her head resting on her knees, she sobbed. Blood and tears soaked her jeans, her whole face throbbed, as did her scalp.

Sitting in the darkness, Kim was reliving the viciousness of the attack. After seeing the dagger, the seriousness of her situation, became chillingly obvious. Janu was capable of anything. She had referred to Tom. "Did she know him? Had she been at Elysium? Had he told her where she lived?" A thousand unanswered questions were spinning round her head. Finally Kim's sobbing subsided and feeling around in the darkness for something to wipe her injured face, her shaking hand came upon the picnic hamper. Carefully opening the lid, she groped around inside. On finding a packet of paper napkins, she pulled some out and gently dabbed her nose and mouth, both of which were badly swollen. The temperature in the cupboard was considerably lower than in the house. Kim realised she was shivering badly probably from a combination of the cold and shock. Groping around she found one of Tom's old fleeces. Wrapping it around her shoulders, she could still smell a faint trace of his favourite aftershave. The smell triggered another fit of sobbing,

Hours passed, slow miserable hours, during which, Kim hadn't heard a sound. Suddenly the door flew open, Kim screwed up her eyes against the brightness. Janu stood staring at her for a few minutes, and then she began to laugh, shaking her head and pointing down at her. "If only Tom could see his darling wife now, he wouldn't think you so special" she said "You are pathetic" Kim pushed herself further back into the cupboard, she felt terrified, yet at the same time, humiliated. "Get out" Janu yelled, grabbing Kim's wrist so tightly, her nails dug into her flesh. Kim pleaded with her, not to hurt her again. This only made Janu laugh all the more; she was obviously enjoying making Kim suffer.

She began to drag her victim upstairs, Kim tried feebly, to resist, but Janu raised her fist to threaten her and Kim had no option but to comply. Once upstairs Janu kicked Adam's bedroom door open and half pushed, half threw, Kim inside. In the centre of Janu's circle on the floor, there were now three rudimentary dolls. They were about eighteen inches tall. The bodies and heads were made out of what looked like hessian and the arms and legs were made of twigs. Two of the dolls lay side by side; the third was propped up in a standing position at their feet. The doll in the upright position had what appeared to be a lock of Janu's hair on its head. One of the dolls lying at its feet had, to Kim's horror, a lock of her own hair. Draped across its chest was a gold crucifix she recognised as the one Tom had given to her last Christmas. The third doll had a photograph of Tom's face on it. Kim could tell immediately, it was one from her wedding album.

Screaming, Kim made an attempt to run out of the room. Before she could reach the door, Janu's arms were round her waist in a bear hug. She seemed to lift her effortlessly and squeezed her so tight, she couldn't breathe. Kim could feel the room spinning as she began to loose consciousness.

CHAPTER 27

CANNABRAE

Kevin McLeod fed his cattle twice a day: between seven and eight in the morning, then again between five and six in the evening. To reach the field he would drive his tractor past the driveway to Bluebell Cottage. Over the past week Kevin had noticed there had been no tracks in the snow to or from Kim's home. On a couple of occasions he'd toyed with the idea of going up to see if everything was okay. He knew Kim's husband had left her to join some kind of hippie commune. This information he had gleaned from the postie, who thrived on all the local gossip. The chap was only too glad to share any new information, concerning the locals, to anyone who was prepared to listen. Kevin didn't really care about the local gossip, but being polite and well mannered he would listen patiently.

At the exact time that Kim was loosing consciousnesses that Friday evening, Kevin was driving past the track to Bluebell Cottage. As he drove past, he made up his mind to call in on the way home, to check Kim was okay. On arriving at the field he opened the gate and drove in, closing the gate behind him. The cattle waited patiently as he lowered the bale from his front loader. The lights from the tractor allowed him to have a quick look at the herd: all present and correct. Climbing back into the tractor, he drove to the gate, opened it and then drove through. After closing the gate, he set off for Kim's cottage.

On reaching Kim's house, Kevin noticed there were lights on both upstairs and downstairs, the jeep was covered with snow and he could also see smoke coming from the chimney. "Definitely someone in" he thought. As he leaned forward to turn off the ignition, his mobile phone rang. On answering it, he was dismayed to hear Archie Fraser, from the neighbouring farm, give him the news, that some of his cattle were loose on the road. Archie said he had tried to herd the cows back into the field himself but unfortunately, they had panicked and gone off in different directions. Kevin thanked him, saying he'd be there in five minutes. Turning quickly, he set off back down the track.

On arriving at the field, Kevin could see Archie's car ahead of him with the hazard lights flashing. Kevin pulled up about thirty yards before the field entrance. The two men closed in on the cattle, driving them through the open gate. Kevin closed the gate and checked the catch. As he suspected, there was nothing wrong with the mechanism. In fact, he had replaced the gate only a few months earlier. Both men were puzzled at how the gate had become opened. Neither of them believed anyone would have done such a thing deliberately. The only logical explanation was that Kevin himself hadn't closed it properly. Kevin thanked Archie then both men went their separate ways. On his way home Kevin drove past Kim's road end but decided not to return this evening as it was getting late. Instead he would call in tomorrow after he'd fed his cattle. Being Saturday he would be going into town for his weekly shopping. If indeed there was a reason she was unable to go out, he could get her any provisions she needed.

Arriving at the farm, Kevin went inside. Feeling rather hungry, he opened the freezer and taking out a shepherd's pie, he popped it in the microwave. While waiting for his meal to cook, he made some tea. When everything was ready, he sat on the armchair beside the Aga, to eat his meal. He began to think about the open gate. "Did he really forget to close it?" He quickly discounted this, from an early age, closing gates, became second nature to everyone in the farming community.

Kevin began to reminisce about his childhood. Although growing up on a farm was hard work, Kevin loved every minute of it. In those days, farming was very different from what it is today. His father, Jock, had his own dairy herd, which of course needed to be milked twice a day. After this, the byre had to be mucked out and everything hosed down, which was one of Kevin's jobs. There were no days off; the milking had to be done 365 days of the year. Jock also had a flock of about 100 hardy black-faced ewes. Lambing time meant Jock would be working round the clock. Pigs were reared for slaughter, normally between four and six at one time. Jock performed the grisly task himself and he would also butcher the carcasses. Some of the meat would be put in the freezer, the rest sold to the local butchers. Jock had a natural ability as a dog trainer. He usually kept four or five collies at any one time, each one at varying stages of their training. He often bred from his best dogs and sold the puppies. His mother, Jessie, looked after the dairy. It was kept so clean you could have eaten your dinner off the floor. At lambing time, the orphan lambs would be bottle-fed by Jessie, often weak or sickly lambs were brought into the house: the warmth from the AGA stove saved many lambs from certain death. Jessie kept a flock of hens, selling any excess eggs. She was also an expert beekeeper, with three beehives, that provided enough honey for the family, with always a little left over for sale. The only other animals on the farm were the cats, employed to keep down the rats and mice. How good life had been back then. If only he and Anna had been blessed with children, to carry on the family tradition. He shook his head, as if to clear its thoughts and decided to have an early night. Tomorrow he would make sure Kim was okay. Thinking about his neighbour helped him feel more positive, as every time he thought about Anna he could feel himself sinking into a depressive state.

CHAPTER 28

THE RITUAL

Janu unceremoniously dumped Kim on the floor. As her lungs filled with oxygen, Kim regained consciousness. Just then both women heard the loud noise of Kevin's tractor approaching. Janu quickly reached into her pocket and pulled out the dagger. Pushing Kim backwards onto the floor she straddled her chest. Pushing the blade into her throat, almost enough to draw blood, she warned her not to make a sound. Kim's mind was racing. "Should she start screaming?" If she put up enough of a struggle, maybe Kevin could get into the house in time to save her life and maybe this would be her only chance of escape. Kim decided to wait until he was at the door, as every second would count. To Kim's utter dismay, not only did he not come to the door, he didn't even stop the tractor. Her heart sank as she heard him turn around and the sound of his tractor fading into the night. Janu laughed triumphantly. "My spells are certainly working!" she said. "Bullshit! You crazy bitch!" retorted Kim. For this she received a painful backhand across her already swollen mouth.

Pulling Kim by the hair to an upright position Janu sat her in the corner. Taking each doll in turn she began to explain the significance of them individually. The doll in the upright position was Janu herself; she called it the"Domini". The doll that represented Kim was the "Essence" and finally, Tom's was the "Vessel". She then produced the book Kim had seen her reading previously: it was titled "Ritual Magic". She informed Kim; that since arriving, she had been performing rituals throughout the house. Also during her stay, she had been absorbing Kim's essence. She explained that when her rituals were complete at the cottage and she had absorbed enough of Kim's essence, she would return to Elysium and carry out the final phase of the ritual. This would be the merging of the Vessel with the Essence. Noticing the puzzled expression on Kim's face, she explained, that Tom being the "Vessel", would be drawn to the "Essence". "Tom! What the Hell has Tom got to do with all this!" Kim screamed. Janu told her how, for the last few months she had been living with Tom: sharing a bed with him, in a yurt. Being "best friends" he had told her all the intimate details of his life and now the only thing that stood in the way of their future happiness, was Kim.

Tears began streaming down Kim's face, she felt completely hopeless. She was going to die, probably a slow, painful death, knowing the woman who was taking her life was also taking her husband. Janu pulled Kim to her feet and dragged her in to the bathroom. Closing the door, she began running the bath. She turned to Kim and in a hard unnatural voice, ordered her to strip and get into the bath. Obediently, Kim followed her instruction, as if in an automatic daze. Throwing a sponge at her, Janu told Kim, to clean up her face. As Kim washed herself, Janu stood over her watching impatiently. After Kim had washed herself, Janu instructed her to get out, throwing a towel at her. Leading her into Kim's bedroom, she told her to get dressed. Kim put on a jogging suit and a pair of trainers. After dressing she sat on the bed and buried her face in her hands sobbing. Meanwhile Janu opened Kim's wardrobe and began throwing items of clothing out onto the floor. Next, all her shoes and handbags got the same treatment. The room was soon littered with all of Kim's beautiful belongings. Finding a large cardboard box on the top shelf, Janu opened it and shrieked with delight. Kim glanced up as Janu danced about the room, holding Kim's wedding dress against her body. "This is perfect" she squealed, as she quickly began undressing. Changing into the dress, she was overjoyed at how well it fitted her. Kim sat in numbed silence watching her. Apart from the length it fitted her perfectly, Kim thought bitterly. Pulling Kim to her feet, she once again dragged her into Adam's room. After pushing her roughly on to the floor in the far corner, Janu opened up the book of rituals and began to chant. Picking up the dolls that represented herself and Tom, she bound them together with silver braid. All the while Kim sat in the corner, terrified to speak or move, convinced at any moment, she was going to be sacrificed.

Suddenly the chanting stopped and Janu collapsed onto the floor. She began thrashing around, her eyes rolled back in their sockets and she started to make deep grumbling noises as saliva drooled from her mouth. Kim sat for a few seconds watching her in absolute terror. Janu seemed totally oblivious to everything. Deciding this could be her only chance to escape, slowly Kim got up. There was no response. She took a few steps and there was, still no response. Carefully, she stepped over Janu and slipped out of the door. Janu continued to thrash around on the floor.

Kim raced downstairs. She didn't try the doors, as she was sure they would be locked. Opening the sitting room window, she grabbed Gemini and climbed out into the darkness. Running now for her life, Kim set off down the drive. Thankfully, Kevin's tractor tracks made it easier underfoot. She had only gone fifty yards and already her trainers and jogging trousers were soaked. Carrying the dog was also slowing her down considerably. Due to shortness of breath the running had slowed to a jog. Kim considered putting Gemini down. She quickly discounted this, knowing he would become disorientated in the strange environment and there was also a good chance he might return to the cottage. If that happened, she didn't dare think what would become of him. With this in mind, Kim had no option but to continue carrying the dog.

She thought about Janu thrashing around on the floor. Could she be an epileptic? If so, Kim hoped she would swallow her tongue and choke to death. Or was that just an urban myth? Nearing the end of the drive, Kim stopped to catch her breath. Suddenly she heard footsteps in the snow behind her. Diving quickly off the track, she crouched down behind a gorse bush. Hardly daring to breath she sat motionless, waiting, as the footsteps drew closer, convinced that at any second Janu would appear. Peering through the bush Kim almost laughed with relief as a roe deer appeared.

Setting off again at a steady jog, she soon reached the tarmac road. Thankfully the snowplough had been and the road was clear. This made it much easier underfoot and she began to pick up speed. A few hundred yards down the road, again, she had to slow down to catch her breath. Her arms were aching with the weight of the dog. Kim had no option but to put him down and Gemini hopped along beside her. Walking briskly along the road, she prayed that a car would come along soon, otherwise it was going to be a long two miles to Kevin's farm. The dog seemed to be coping all right: she decided if a car came along, she would pick him up.

Half a mile further on, she stopped and straining her ears, she thought she could hear a car approaching. Sure enough, headlights swept round the curve of the road. Bending down, she picked up Gemini. Kim was ecstatic; at last she would be saved. Standing in the middle of the road, she began to flag the car down. The car slowed to a stop a few feet from her.

After the darkness, she was blinded with the bright headlamps. As Kim rushed towards the vehicle, the door opened and a tall figure emerged wearing a long coat and flat cap. Kim threw her arms around the driver, but immediately she sensed something was wrong. Before she had a chance to break free, she felt a metal chain around her neck. Janu tugged mercilessly on what was, in fact, Pepsi's choke chain.

In a desperate attempt to escape, Kim dropped the little dog, which landed on the ground with a yelp and ran off into the darkness. It was useless, Kim was already exhausted and after a brief struggle, Janu once again, overpowered her. Kim put up little resistance, as Janu dragged her by the chain, to the back of the Jeep. With a vicious tug, she pulled her head down and fastened the choke chain to the tow bar. Kim's head was only inches away from the exhaust pipe. The fumes, coupled with the tight chain around her neck, were suffocating her. From her pocket Janu produced a roll of duct tape and working quickly, she taped Kim's wrists together, behind her back. Her ankles were then tied in the same manner. Janu rummaged about in the boot, until she found a rag and forcing Kim's jaws apart, stuffed the gag in to her mouth. Muffled cries of pain could be heard, as Janu heartlessly wrapped the tape around Kim's swollen and tender mouth.

Once satisfied, she untied the choke chain. As she did this, Kim collapsed on to the road. Janu effortlessly picked the helpless woman up and callously dumped her into the boot, slamming the lid down noisily. All went quiet and the minutes ticked by until the sound of footsteps could be heard coming towards the vehicle. Suddenly, the boot flew open and a wet and bedraggled Gemini was thrown in to the space beside her. Kim lay on her side, desperately trying to breath through her bruised and bloodied nose. She could feel the Jeep being manoeuvred, as Janu turned and drove back to Bluebell Cottage, singing and laughing triumphantly.

CHAPTER 29

AN EVENING ALONE

February found Elysium, covered in a blanket of thick snow. All out door work had been suspended. The interior work carried on as normal. Floor boards that had became rotten, due to the rain and damp coming through the broken windows, were being ripped out and replaced. Alex had been assigned to help with this task. One morning, Tom, Gina and little Becky were preparing food in the yurt, when Alex returned from work early. His brother had arrived, bearing bad news about their mother. The old lady had suffered a stroke and was gravely ill. Alex began packing some things into suitcases for the children and himself. He asked Tom and Gina if they would mind looking after Gemini for a few days. Gina and Tom readily agreed to take care of the dog.

Once Alex and the children had left, Tom suggested they take Gemini for a walk. They had walked for about an hour, when the snow began to fall quite heavily and they decided to head home. By the time they got back to the yurt, they were both soaked through. Once inside,

Tom rubbed Gemini down with a towel, to dry him off. Next, he turned his attention to the stove, filling it up with firewood. He was so engrossed in what he was doing, it wasn't until he looked up, that he saw Gina standing completely naked by her bed, drying herself. Tom blushed, apologising and turned away. Gina laughed, teasingly. "Don't be shy" she said, "after all, we are almost a married couple".

Tom quickly put on his jacket, excusing himself, saying he would get more fuel for the stove. When he returned a while later, neither of them mentioned the incident. That evening, as they sat by the fire, Tom asked Gina about her childhood. She told him, she had been an only child and both her parents had been professionals. Often, both of them were absent, or on business for long periods. Her nanny had been more of a parent to her, than her mother or father. On the rare occasions they were at home, they would be hosting dinner parties, or attending social events. The incident with her dog had affected her profoundly, causing her to have terrible nightmares for months. She also became afraid, to venture out of the house alone. Her nanny would accompany her to and from school, every day. She seldom left the house and subsequently, became isolated from the other children in the vicinity. She became a loner. Tom felt a wave of sympathy towards her, he himself had come from a close and loving family.

It was after midnight when they both retired to bed. Tom felt slightly awkward that night, not having Alex and the children in the yurt. It was strange, being alone with a young woman, both of them lying so close in the stillness. As he settled down to sleep, his thoughts turned to Kim, as they did every night. "How he missed her". Eventually, he fell in to a deep sleep. Some time through the night, he became aware of Gina lying in bed with him. Her arm was across his chest. As he slowly began to slide away, her arm tightened, preventing him from moving further. Gina suddenly pulled herself against him and her lips became merged with his, in a passionate kiss. Taken aback, Tom put his hands on her shoulders. Gently but firmly, he pushed her away. He tried to explain his feelings. He was flattered that such a beautiful young woman was attracted to him but it could not be. He enjoyed her company immensely, but he was still deeply in love with his wife, Kim. Gina lay silent for a few minutes before she slid out from under the covers and returned to her own bed. Tom breathed a sigh of relief. He lay there, thinking in the darkness.

Some time in the night, he came to a decision, Elysium was not for him and he belonged with Kim. Tomorrow he would leave the place and return to his wife, if that is, she would have him, though he couldn't blame her if she would not. He spent a restless night, wondering if she would take him back after all this time. For all he knew, she could have found someone else. Then there was Gorda, they had become good friends." How would he explain it to him?" Last, but by no means least, "How would Gina react?" After all, it was obvious she had become very attached, even a little dependent on him. Just before dawn, he fell asleep.

He was awakened by the sound of Gina preparing breakfast. After getting dressed, he approached her gingerly. She was buttering the toast and had her back to him. After wishing her "Good morning!" he apologised for the previous night. He began by putting the blame on himself, for giving her the 'wrong signals'. He went on to say, that after breakfast, he would tell Gorda, he planned to leave the Fellowship and return to Kim. Gina made no response, she stood perfectly still throughout Tom's speech, never uttering a sound. After a very strained and pregnant pause, Tom reached out gently, to touch her shoulder, apologising once again.

Gina spun around. He felt the wind being knocked out of him. He thought she had punched him and looked down, in time to see Gina pull a bloodied dagger out of his stomach. His legs suddenly began to feel strangely weak. He looked up questioningly into Gina's eyes, eyes that seemed to pierce his soul with hatred, he would never forget. His hand had dropped instinctively to where he had been struck, and now felt warm and sticky. Looking down he could see dark red blood oozing out between his fingers. As his legs buckled under him, he managed to mutter a puzzled "Why" before the ground rushed up to meet him. He felt cold and numb and realised he was lying on the floor and going in to shock. He was vaguely aware of Gemini coming and going from his field of vision, barking loudly. Just before he lost consciousness, he saw Gina grab her rucksack, pick up the little dog and holding his mouth shut, rush out of the yurt.

CHAPTER 30

CONFESSIONS

On arriving back at the cottage, Janu carried the dog into the house, before returning for her hostage. Hauling Kim out of the car, she dumped her on the snow and moved around behind her. She put her arms around Kim's chest and dragged her backwards into the sitting room, propping her up on the armchair beside the fire. Janu began to pace around the room in an agitated state, ranting and raving. She blamed Tom and Kim for everything she had done to them. She said they had driven her to it. She told Kim, that Tom had come on to her and when she responded, he had rejected her. She continued saying it was his own fault that she had stabbed him and he had brought it on himself. She had, however, forgiven him and when the ritual was complete, he would be hers forever.

Kim listened with dumb amazement; she couldn't quite take it all in. This woman had stabbed Tom. Her brain was telling her to ask if he was okay, but she could only make muffled noises through the gag in her mouth. The sound of the phone ringing startled her.

Janu warned her not to make a sound. In a surprisingly calm voice, Janu told the caller; that Kim gone to Elysium to see Tom and would be gone for some time. As the conversation progressed, Kim realised it was Nicola phoning from New Zealand. Janu went on to explain that she had been employed to house sit for the duration of Kim's absence.

After hanging up, Janu came over to Kim, saying, "Since you have been a good girl, we will take that dirty old rag out of your mouth." With that, she began unwrapping the tape from around her prisoner's face. Kim could not prevent herself from crying in pain, as some of her hair came away with the tape as it was being removed. Her mouth had also begun to bleed again, with the release of the pressure. Janu noticed this, and dipped her index finger into some of the blood that trickled down her chin. Kim stared wide-eyed in disbelief, as her captor studied it for a few seconds, before licking it from her finger. Seeming to be much calmer now, Janu sat opposite her on the couch. As if she was on a social call, she 'matter of factly' explained that the phone had never been out of order, all she had done was unplug it. The fact that the socket was hidden behind the bookshelves, made it so easy. She had phoned the veterinary practice; giving them the same story she had given Nicola. The jeep had been just as easy; all she had done was disconnect the battery. Kim cursed herself for not checking any of these obvious things, before everything had got out of hand. Now it was too late.

Janu left the room for a few minutes, returning with what appeared to be a tray covered with snow. After placing it in front of the fire, she sat cross-legged beside it, with her ritual book lying open. Kim noticed the snow had a zigzag pattern pressed into it. After a few seconds she realised it was tyre print of Kevin's tractor. Even by Janu's standards, this was bizarre, she thought, her mind racing. "What could this mean?"

She watched, as the woman placed her dagger in the centre of the snow covered tray and begin to chant. The heat from the fire quickly melted the snow, until all that was left, was a pool of muddy water. When Janu came to the end of her chant, she picked up the dagger and sat with her eyes closed for several minutes. Then she picked up the tray and hurled the contents into the fire, which seemed to explode with a loud hiss, spitting out steam, water and ash over the two women. As Kim cowered from the deluge, Janu raised the dagger triumphantly in the air. "So be it!" she cried.

Janu cut the duct tape from around Kim's ankles pulled off her trainers and led her upstairs. Kim began shaking uncontrollably, convinced this was the end. Instead of taking her into Adams room, she was led to the bathroom. Feeling totally helpless, Janu pulled down her joggers and gently guided her on to the loo. Her demeanour had changed yet again. Using a face cloth, she gently, almost lovingly, washed Kim's swollen and bloodied face. Next she was led into her own bedroom and instructed to sit on the bed. After sifting around the clothes strewn on the floor, Janu picked out a pair of pyjamas. She gently helped Kim out of her soiled clothes and on with the new ones. Leading her over to the bed, she pulled back the covers and signalled for her to get in. Obediently Kim did as she was told. As she lay down, Janu produced a silk scarf. She tied Kim's wrist with one end and the other she fastened to the headboard. Then to Kim's horror, she climbed into bed and snuggled up against her.

She lay there, afraid to move, as Janu began to stroke her hair. Despite herself, Kim was grateful for the warmth coming from the woman, as she had never been so cold in all her life. She lay there perfectly still, not daring to move, lest she set Janu off on a tirade again. Outside the rain could be heard lashing against the window. Janu continued to stroke her hair, whispering almost to herself. "Not long now, it will soon be over. Even the weather is under my control, my power increases every day". Kim didn't respond, she was too exhausted and afraid. Her only hope was that Kevin would return tomorrow.

CHAPTER 31

FEEDING TIME

On Saturday morning, Kevin awoke at his normal time, 7 am. Once dressed, he went downstairs. Looking out, he could see that, due to the heavy rain, the snow had almost disappeared. He made tea and toast and sat down, listening to the radio, as he did every morning. By eight he had collected a bale of hay on the front loader and set off to feed the cattle. Slowing down as he passed Bluebell Cottage he could see faint tracks left in the slush, but was unsure if they were his or if another vehicle had been there. He decided to put his mind at rest and call in after he had fed the cattle. Not long afterwards he pulled the tractor to a halt at the field. He jumped out of the cab and opened the gate, rubbing his hands together. "There's still a nip in the air." he thought. Driving the machine into the field, he alighted once more to close the gate. The cattle as normal, were patiently awaiting his arrival. He dipped the forks and lowered the bale to the ground. Once again, he stepped down out of the tractor, feeling in his pocket for the knife he used to cut the twine. He neither saw nor heard the young bull, coming at a charge behind him. The first thing he knew, was the impact of the beast's head smashing into his lower back, as it crushed him against the hay ring. Shocked and winded he turned around, unable to prevent it charging a second time, pinning him, once again against the steel, pushing the air out of his lungs, crushing his ribs and smashing his internal organs. He could hear and feel the snapping of bones as he collapsed to the ground, in agony. Stabbing pains in his back, made it impossible for him to return to his feet. Cursing himself, for not carrying whis mobile, he looked around frantically, for some means of escape.

The enraged animal prepared for another onslaught, its eyes wide and glazed. Steam billowed from its flaring nostrils as it pawed at the ground, sending sprays of muddy water into the air. Holding on to the hay ring, he tried, once again, to pull himself to his feet, it was no use. Severe pain travelled down both of his legs, from his injured back. Crawling now, he tried to make it to the safety of the tractor. Suddenly, he was pushed violently into the ground, screaming in pain, as his arm was caught in an unnatural angle, before it snapped at the wrist. He could feel the wet muddy ground soaking his overalls and he collapsed back into the mire. He was having difficulty breathing, as his pierced lungs began to fill with fluid.

The bullock stood pawing the ground and tossing its head. Kevin had never seen any of his herd behave in such a manner and he had reared these animals from calves. The rest of the herd seemed oblivious to what was going on and had begun eating the hay as normal. It just didn't make sense. His breathing was becoming more laboured, his body felt cold, a numbness starting at his feet was travelling up through his entire body. The young bull seemed to tire of his quarry and wandered off back to the rest of the herd.

Again Kevin tried to move, but his body would not respond. Gasping now for breath, the realisation struck him, that this was the end. His head fell back, once again, into the mud. He neither had the energy nor the will to try to escape. As he lay there, a feeling of peace began to come over him. A strangely familiar sense of relief was growing within him. The sadness and despair, that had become such an integral part of him, had vanished. The hopeless feeling of being alone, that he had lived with so long, had gone. There was no more pain, no more gasping for breath. He thought he heard his beloved Anna, calling to him. Yes, she was there, smiling, holding out her hand to him, her eyes bright with joy. Tears of happiness came to his eyes and smiling he went to meet his darling Anna, once again.

Chapter 32

The Wood Shed

At the same time that Kevin was drawing his last breath. Janu and Kim were getting out of bed. They went down stairs and into the kitchen. Janu sat Kim down at the kitchen table and tied her hands securely to the chair. Then as if all was normal, she said she would make them both a coffee. Shortly, she returned and untied one of Kim's hands to allow her to drink the dark liquid. Kim wondered if she should attempt to throw the hot coffee over her captor. Deciding against it, she solemnly began sipping the brew. Janu then surprised her, by announcing, she was going into town. Kim and Gemini were to be locked in the wood shed for the duration of her absence.

After tying Kim's hands behind her back, she led her out of the cottage, towards the outhouse. The building was adjacent to the house; it was stone built and had a corrugated iron roof. When they were inside the building, Janu used the duct tape once again, wrapping it tightly around Kim's ankles. Next, she covered her mouth with it. She stood for a minute, smiling at the sight of her prisoner, trussed up, immobile and looking helpless. She seemed to find the sight amusing and then came a step closer. With the same gloating smile, she extended one finger and prodded Kim, who unbalanced and toppled over onto the woodpile. Gemini was then pushed inside and the wooden door closed and locked. The only light came from a two-inch gap at the bottom of the door.

Kim made herself as comfortable as she could, lying there in the gloom, once more a prisoner. Under normal circumstances, being bound, gagged and confined in the dark, would have terrified her. To her surprise, she was perfectly calm. Then she realised, a week had gone by: a week of living in constant fear, tension and humiliation. How she hated the woman who had put her through this nightmare. "Well at least for the time being, the bitch is not here terrorising me." She thought. She experienced another wave of relief when she heard the Jeep start up and the engine grow fainter as it faded into the distance.

For the first few minutes Kim lay there motionless, before manoeuvring herself into a sitting position. The will to survive seemed to have deserted her; she had given up all hope of escape. Gemini's scratching caught her attention. The little dog was frantically trying to dig his way out under the door. Kim sighed dejectedly, even if he did mange to dig a hole deep enough inside the building, it was pointless. They would never get by the concrete paving on the outside. As she watched his futile attempt, her eye caught sight of the key hole. There was no light shining through, this could mean only one thing-the key was still in the lock. Kim stood up quickly, almost losing her balance, forgetting the tape around her ankles. If she could push the key out onto the paving, maybe, with a lot of luck, she could somehow manage to retrieve it and unlock the door.

Suddenly her will to survive, returned with a vengeance. "Think. Stay calm." she told herself. First she had to find something with which to push the key out of the lock. Sitting back down on to her bottom, she began to feel around on the dirt floor, for a splinter of wood long enough, to dislodge the key. This task was made all the more difficult, with her hands tied behind her back. The floor was littered with years of sawdust, bark and pieces of wood.

After numerous failed attempts, she finally found a suitable piece. She paused concerned the key would fall beyond her reach and remembered the cardboard box in the corner where old newspapers were stored to light the fire. Sliding backwards she toppled the box onto its side. Groping through the papers, many of which were damp, her hand felt the shiny cover of a magazine. This would be perfect for the task.

Kim was finding it hard to breath. The exertion combined with the restriction of the gag, was making her feel light-headed. She decided she would, somehow, have to remove the tape from over her mouth. Taking drastic action, she began to rub the duct tape on her face, against the stone wall. She could feel the rough stone scratching her skin as she moved her head up and down. She believed; if she could just get it loosened a little, she would be able to work it down from her mouth. Alternating from one side of her face to the other, the tape began to come away from her skin. Slowly it began to curl up at the sides, until at last it began to roll down her cheeks. After what seemed like an eternity, her mouth was finally free of the tape. She had paid a high price for this, as both her cheeks were badly grazed. Realising a major obstacle had just been removed, she leaned against the wall, taking large gulps of air, enjoying the feeling of being able to breath again.

Elated with her progress, she carefully edged the magazine under the door, turning around periodically to check her progress. Conscious of the time Janu had been gone. She realised it was possible Janu could return any time. Clasping the splinter in her hand, she managed to get herself upright. Shuffling backwards until her hands touched the door, carefully she felt along the door until her hand and then finger found the keyhole. Praying inwardly, she tentatively inserted the splinter into the keyhole. She could hardly contain her excitement, when she heard a dull clunk, as the key landed on the magazine. Sliding down the door onto her bottom again, she rolled onto her side to look under the door. Sure enough, the key had landed perfectly a few inches from the door. Using both hands, slowly inch by inch, she pulled the paper underneath the door. Time was of the essence now. Holding the key tightly, she stood up. Backing up against the door, her other hand soon found the keyhole. Kim slid the key into the lock and turned, the door opened.

She knew she wasn't out of the woods yet: she had to free her hands. She hopped around the side of the buildings, hoping to find something sharp enough to cut the tape. Finding nothing, she quickly began rubbing her wrists up against the corner of one of the buildings. Sawing through the tape was causing her wrists to suffer the same fate as her face. As the stonework cut through the tape it also removed a layer of skin from her wrists. A few minutes later her hands were free. Bending down Kim quickly unwrapped the tape from around her ankles. In the distance she heard the familiar sound of her Jeep. Having got this far, she was determined; she was not going to give in without a fight.

She would need to find a weapon. Glancing quickly around the outbuilding, her eyes fell upon an old axe handle. This would have to do." It's a pity the axe head is missing." She thought. Kim visualised herself plunging the axe into Janu's skull. Closing and locking the door, she raced to the corner of the cottage. Positioning herself, her weapon raised in anticipation, she waited. Kim felt remarkably calm; she was almost looking forward to the confrontation and for the first time she had the upper hand plus the element of surprise.

CHAPTER 33

THE FINAL RITUAL

As Janu drove back from town, tucked safely in her pocket, was her Sodium Valproate. Since early childhood she had suffered from epilepsy and normally she was careful not to run out of her medication but she had used so many of her pills to drug Kim, that it had depleted her supply. The result being she had ran out yesterday causing last night's seizure. This could not happen tonight, when she would be performing the final ritual. The sacrifice of Kim would be the culmination of all her efforts. As she was driving, she ran through her plan. After she had sacrificed Kim, she would take her downstairs, lay her on the sofa and place a couple of empty wine bottles beside her. Then she would set the house alight, making it appear to have been started by a hot ember falling out of the fire. The house was so far out of town, that by the time the fire brigade arrived, there wouldn't be much left of her. This would make determining the cause of death, all the more difficult. She would take the dog with her in the jeep, to a secluded spot. There she would bludgeon him to death and toss him over the nearest bridge. After travelling a suitable distance she would torch the vehicle. She would then head back to Elysium. Tom would not be able to resist her, as by then she would have absorbed all of Kim's essence. The circle would then be complete.

Smiling at her perfect plan, Janu pulled up at the cottage. Getting out of the jeep, she quickly looked around the front of the house, looking for any signs of disturbance. Feeling confident and with a spring in her step, she walked towards the house. She paused at the front door and then appeared to change her mind, heading to the rear. She rounded the corner to check on her captive and with a sickening thud, the axe handle smashed against her head. She fell backwards, hitting her head against the wall. Blood smeared the wall as she slowly slid to the ground. Kim was triumphant, wondering if she had actually killed her. Still armed with the axe handle she cautiously approached Janu's limp body and crouching, began to check for any signs of life. To her utter amazement the woman still had a weak pulse. Searching through Janu's pockets, she found the car keys. She ran towards the jeep, almost forgetting Gemini. After calling for him a couple of times, the little dog emerged from under the privet hedge. Picking him up, she climbed into the jeep. Once inside, not taking any chances, she clicked down the central locking button. She turned the key and the engine roared into action. Slamming into reverse gear Kim swung the car round and was gone. She was laughing, crying, shouting and screaming as the jeep bounced down the drive.

CHAPTER 34

JANU GINAHAUSEN

It had been ten days since Tom had been admitted to hospital. He had under gone an emergency operation on arrival as well as receiving 2 pints of blood. After Gina's vicious attack in the yurt, he had lain unconscious for about twenty minutes. Thankfully, one of Becky's friends had called round to take Gemini for a walk. Tom was to discover later, due to the amount of blood he had lost, coupled with shock.That the little girls calls of alarm, had saved his life.

After being admitted into the hospital, the police had been alerted. Tom had been too ill to give a statement. However, from the information they received from other members of the commune, a thorough search out of the yurt was immediately carried out. They removed everything that belonged to Gina, for examination. While going through her belongings, a birth certificate was found with the name Janu Ginahausen, date of birth 08.06.74: place of birth, Salzburg. She had only been in the United Kingdom for eight months.

On contacting the Austrian Police, Gina/Janu's history began to unfold. Her earlier life had been spent in a series of orphanages, beginning in 1976, after her mother, who was a registered heroin addict, could no longer care for her. From the age of seven, she had been in numerous foster homes. By the time she was thirteen, she had already been in trouble with the authorities. At the age of nineteen she began her first prison sentence for drug trafficking. Over the next fifteen years, she served a number of short prison sentences. The crimes ranged from petty theft, drug trafficking, fraud and soliciting.

A year before leaving the country, her life seemed to have settled down. She was living with her boyfriend in a fourth floor flat in Vienna. However, in the early hours of Saturday, the twenty first of June, two thousand and nine the police were called to an apartment in Vienna, concerning what appeared to have been a fatal accident. A young man had died, after falling from a fourth floor balcony. His then girlfriend had been in the house at the time of the accident. When questioned, she said, she was in bed asleep at the time of the incident. She then gave a statement, claiming her boyfriend had been suffering from depression and on a number of occasions, had threatened to commit suicide.

On further investigation, close friends of the young man denied these allegations. Due to insufficient evidence, they released the young woman, Janu Gina-hausen, until they received the results of the post mortem. A week after the death, the results of the post mortem was released. This revealed large traces of Sodium

Valproate, a drug prescribed to epilepsy sufferers. Ginahausen's police record showed an epileptic condition and the authorities believed they now had enough evidence to bring the woman in for further questioning. Unfortunately, when officers returned to the premises, they found it deserted and the woman had disappeared.

CHAPTER 35

A SHOCKING DISCOVERY

On reaching the end of the drive, Kim took a left turn, heading towards town, periodically checking her speed, as the last thing she needed was to crash the car. On reaching the top of a slight incline she saw flashing blue lights. She couldn't believe her luck. There, parked at the side of the road were two police cars and an ambulance.

Elated she drove towards them, but her elation soon turned to dismay. Pulling up parallel to the ambulance she leapt out of the vehicle, just as two medics carried a stretcher through the gateway. Although the head was covered, Kim could see Kevin's tractor still parked in the middle of the field. She shuddered remembering the tray of snow with Kevin's tractor tyre treads on it. "Was Janu responsible for his death? Surely the rituals she performed couldn't actually work! It was all too fantastic: after all we aren't in the dark ages anymore!"

One of the policemen approached her, almost hysterical she began to relate the events of the previous week. She told them how Janu had held her hostage, tortured her, stabbed her husband and she believed was responsible for Kevin's death. Janu, she told them lay badly injured outside Bluebell Cottage the officer seeing her injuries immediately sprang into action.

After radioing for another ambulance and police car, he and his colleague set of in the direction of Kim's home. Meanwhile Kim was escorted to hospital for a check up. Apart from severe bruising and superficial wounds, she had no serious injuries, however the mental scars would take considerably longer to heal. After being discharged Kim phoned her son Adam, asking him to meet her at the police station. Kim pretended there had been a break in and she just needed some moral support.

Without hesitation Adam told her he would set off immediately. Next, she telephoned Stan, the vet. After telling him briefly what had happened, Kim asked if he could take care of Gemini for the night and also check out his injured leg. Stan agreed immediately, saying he would come straight over to the hospital. When Stan arrived to collect the dog he was visibly shocked at the sight of Kim's battered and bruised body. Stan hugged her asking if there was anything else he could do to help. "Just take care of Gemini, it was thanks to him I escaped" she said. The vet followed her to the jeep to retrieve the little dog. Kim stroked him fondly before handing him over.

An hour later Kim and Adam sat in one of the interview rooms at the police station. It took almost three hours for Kim to relate what had taken place over the last nine days of living hell. Often they had to take a break, as Kim would break down. Throughout the interview Adam held his mother's hand, often dabbing his eyes, as he was overcome with emotion at her plight. After the interview was over Kim and Adam booked into a local hotel.

CHAPTER 36

LOOSE ENDS

On arriving at Bluebell Cottage, the two officers went immediately to the rear of the property. This was where Kim had said Janu was lying injured. As they approached the spot it was apparent from the blood splattered wall, as well as the bloodstain on the path, that this was where the confrontation had taken place. Following a trail of blood the officers entered the rear of the house into the kitchen. Lying in a pool of blood there was a woman's body. It was evident from the amount of blood that she was dead. Both her wrists had deep lacerations and in her right hand she still clutched an ornate dagger.

Since arriving at the hotel room, Kim had been in an agitated state, even although she knew there was a policeman outside their door. She couldn't settle, pacing up and down and continually checking that the room door was locked. Adam tried to reassure his mother that she would be safe here with him. The phone ringing made Kim jump, telling Adam not to answer it fearing it may be Janu. Adam gently reassured her, before picking up the receiver. The receptionist informed him she had Tina, one of Kim's work colleagues, with her. She had some items of clothing she thought his mother might need. Adam asked his mother if she was willing to see Tina. Kim hesitated for a few seconds then agreed to see her.

A few minutes later, Tina gently knocked on the door. On entering the room Tina was shocked at the sight of Kim's face. She immediately dropped the bags she was carrying and rushed over to Kim. As she embraced her, both women began to cry. After a few minutes Tina tried to lighten the mood. She explained Stan had called her to tell her what had happened. He asked her if she could think of anything they could do to help. Tina being practical like most woman, suggested they get her some clothes. Guessing Kim would only have the clothes she was wearing when she escaped, Tina had volunteered to nip into Tesco and get enough clothing to tide her over. The two women sat chatting for a few minutes, both avoiding mentioning the events of the previous week.

Once Tina had left Kim emptied the contents of the bags onto the bed. As well as trousers, T-shirts, a jumper, underwear, pyjamas and a bathrobe, was a bag of toiletries. Adam suggested his mother take a shower, while he ordered some food for them. Kim took her new bathrobe and pyjamas and went to the shower room. As she passed the wall mirror she stopped. This was the first opportunity she had had to really study herself. Her face was badly swollen, as was her nose, she had two black eyes and a nasty cut on her upper lip. Worst of all was the imprint in her neck of the choke chain. Each link was so distinct it looked as though someone had drawn it with a marker pen. Once in the shower she began to relax slightly and although it was painful Kim washed herself from head to toe. She wanted every trace of Janu removed from her body. Kim emerged from the shower room wearing her new pyjamas, bathrobe and slippers. A knock at the door sent her scurrying back in, still afraid Janu would appear at any time.

The voice at the other side was one of the officers they had seen earlier. Once the policemen were in the room Kim emerged from the shower room. They informed her that Janu had been pronounced dead on arrival at the hospital. Kim's eyes widened. " Did I kill her?" she asked. One of the officers explained that there would be a post mortem to determine the cause of death, after which, a report would be sent to the Procurator Fiscal. He then divulged, off the record that Janu's wrists had been slashed and when found, she had been clutching an ornate dagger, which matched the description of the one Kim had spoken about.

Up until now Kim had avoided mentioning Kevin, but now that she knew Janu was dead and was therefore, powerless to harm her or her family, her thoughts returned to her neighbour. She asked if they could tell her, how Kevin had died. The officer told her it appeared to have been a tragic accident. Kim wasn't convinced and once again, mentioned the ritual with the snow. Although patient with her, she could see by their expressions, they did not believe Janu had anything to do with Kevin's death.

For the rest of the evening Adam and Kim planned what they would do the next day. Around midnight Kim went to bed and Adam decided to stay with his mother, pulling up an armchair he settled beside her bed. Being in such a fragile state Kim insisted the light be left on. Several times through the night Kim had terrifying nightmares, each time Adam was quickly at her side to reassure her. Eventually he lay on top of the bed beside her, holding her hand.

On Sunday morning after breakfast, Kim and Adam set off to visit Tom in hospital. On the way, they called in at Stan's, to collect little Gemini. Throughout the journey Gemini lay curled up on Kim's knee, while Adam drove the car. By afternoon they were nearing the hospital and Kim told her son, she would like to make a slight detour as there was something she must do before they went to see Tom. Over the next few miles, Kim gave directions until they came to a point in the journey, when Kim asked, " Turn left here". A sign read 'Elysium'.

Although it would be difficult, she had decided to return the little dog to his owner or at least let Gemini decide with whom he wanted to stay. As they travelled down the drive, Gemini began leaping around and waging his tail. The yurt was easy to find and Adam brought the car to a halt beside it. Alex emerged followed by his three children. Kim climbed out of the jeep carrying Gemini. Becky squealed with delight at seeing her dog. Gemini almost leapt out of Kim's arms, running straight towards the child. Well, thought Kim, he has made his choice.

Secretly Kim had been hoping for this outcome. If she had kept him he would have been a constant reminder of her terrifying experience with Janu. Kim introduced Adam and herself to Alex, who in turn invited them both into the yurt for some tea. She declined saying she wanted to see Tom as soon as possible.

From inside the yurt an attractive woman appeared. "Mummy! Mummy! Look who's here" cried Becky. Kim recognised her as one of the women Gorda had chosen. Through the open door Kim caught a glance of suitcases and packed boxes. On seeing Kim's puzzled expression, Alex explained that he, his wife and their family were leaving Elysium. They had decided the Fellowship wasn't for them after all. After a final and tearful goodbye to Gemini Kim and Adam left Elysium forever.

CHAPTER 37

THE REUNION

Walking into the hospital, Kim suddenly felt very nervous. It has been so long since they had seen each other and so much had happened between times. Sensing her apprehension, Adam put a protective arm around her. Due to the severity of Tom's injuries, he was in a room on his own. Together, Kim and Adam entered the room.

Tom was sitting propped up slightly in bed, with his eyes closed. The police had already informed him of his wife's ordeal. Hearing the movement, Tom's eyes fluttered open. Suddenly, he jolted back, at the shock of Kim's injuries. Nothing could have prepared him for the sight he now beheld. He began to weep openly, begging Kim to forgive her everything she had been put through.

Kim rushed over, throwing her arms about him, sobbing uncontrollably. After a few minutes the sobbing subsided a little, as they told one another how lonely the months of separation had been and how they had missed each other more and more as the time had gone on.

When at last, the tearful reunion was over, they began to plan their future. Tom still had many contacts in the property business. They would put Bluebell Cottage on the market immediately. In the meantime, they would rent a property, Edinburgh being their first choice. They would get in touch with Nicola and when Tom had fully recovered, hopefully by August, they would fly out to New Zealand and spend a few months with her. Adam could come over with them during his summer break. If they liked New Zealand, they might even stay. One thing was absolutely certain: neither of them had any intention of returning to the locations, where they had encountered Janu Ginahausen.